DON'T BLEED ON ME

E

T 30

....

PLEASE RETURN TO THE ABOVE LIBRARY OR ANY OTHER ABERDEEN CITY LIBRARY, ON OR BEFORE THE DUE DATE. TO RENEW, PLEASE QUOTE THE DUE DATE AND THE BARCODE NUMBER.

Aberdeen City Council
Library & Information Services

DON'T BLEED ON ME

Basil Copper

This Large Print book is published by BBC Audiobooks Ltd, Bath, England and by Thorndike Press®, Waterville, Maine, USA.

Published in 2005 in the U.K. by arrangement with the author.

Published in 2005 in the U.S. by arrangement with Basil Copper.

U.K. Hardcover   ISBN 1–4056–3367–0 (Chivers Large Print)
U.K. Softcover   ISBN 1–4056–3368–9 (Camden Large Print)
U.S. Softcover   ISBN 0–7862–7677–0 (British Favorites)

The text of this Large Print edition is unabridged.
Other aspects of the book may vary from the original edition.

Set in 16 pt. New Times Roman.

Printed in Great Britain on acid-free paper.

British Library Cataloguing in Publication Data available

Library of Congress Cataloging-in-Publication Data

Copper, Basil.
        Don't bleed on me / by Basil Copper.
            p.   cm.
        "Thorndike Press large print British favorites."—T.p. verso.
        ISBN 0–7862–7677–0 (lg. print : sc : alk. paper)
        1. Faraday, Mike (Fictitious character)—Fiction. 2. Private
        investigators—California—Los Angeles—Fiction.
        3. Government, Resistance to—Fiction. 4. Los Angeles
        (Calif.)—Fiction. 5. Large type books. I. Title.
        PR6053.O658D65 2005
        823'.914—dc22   2005006295

Author's Note

The California of the Mike Faraday novels is a mythical setting, evolved for plot purposes; this includes the weather, geographic and topographical features. It hardly needs emphasizing that the characters are equally fictional. This does not mean to say that the incidents described are not highly probable; in fact many of the incidents described in the books have since come true in a surprisingly parallel manner. While this may be saddening from the point of view of human nature it goes a long way towards explaining Mike Faraday's philosophy on mankind's greed.

B.C.

Contents

Chapter One

Cardinal Bishop

1

It was one of those deceptively golden days in early fall when you begin to think that you'll never again hear from the tax authorities and that human nature has abandoned graft and mayhem. You should know better but the sun and the heat-haze and the benevolent gleam in people's eyes has temporarily conned you and you might perhaps be allowed to forget the darker side. For half an hour, that is.

I was sitting in my office concentrating on a strenuous session of pitching paper clips into my waste basket. Even the air conditioning was working. Which was saying something. It was around lunch-time and I was just thinking of shutting up shop when I heard the reception room door open and close softly. I knew it wasn't Stella because she wasn't due in until early afternoon. Business was slack and that was the arrangement while the heat was off. A shadow materialized against the frosted glass.

'Come in,' I called.

There was a moment's hesitation and then a short, stout party with the most insincere face I'd seen in decades oozed through the

1

doorway. He wore a dark tussore suit that hung limply around his ample poundage; he was a great hunk of man—except that most of it was fat. A thin smear of mustache made a sneering interruption between his nose and his mouth; two gold teeth winked ingratiatingly from between his lips. His eyebrows were Mephistophelean. His close-cropped sandy hair made the top of his head look like a toilet brush.

'Mr Faraday?' His voice was soft and womanish. He twisted his green pork-pie hat in sweating hands. I admitted it. The fat man sank into the chair I indicated; he mopped a greasy brow with a red-bordered handkerchief he took from his rear pants pocket. 'We're in the same line of business, Mr Faraday.'

'You surprise me,' I said.

The fat man blinked; he looked the type that was used to scarcely veiled denigration. He produced a dirty piece of pasteboard from a cheap imitation crocodile-skin wallet and slid it across the desk at me.

I held it between my thumb and forefinger. It said; Cardinal Bishop; and underneath, Private Investigations —Divorce a Speciality. I'll bet I said to myself. I put the card back on my blotter and waited for him to speak. He didn't so the move was up to me.

'What can I do for you, Mr Bishop?' I said.

The fat man blinked again. He ran a blue-pink tongue round his plump lower lip. 'I've run into a little trouble, Mr Faraday. Strong-arm action. It's a bit out of my line.'

'So you farm out the muscle stuff,' I said. 'So long as it's legal.'

Cardinal Bishop lowered his pouchy eyelids over his insincere eyes and tried to look as if my suggestion had pained him. 'It's legal,' he said.

I studied his card again. 'With a name like that you ought to be in the church,' I said.

Mr Bishop went pink around his fat ears and he rolled his eyes once or twice. I guessed he had heard it all before.

'No jokes about my name, Mr Faraday,' he mumbled. He wiped his forehead again, transferring more grease to his handkerchief.

'This is serious. I thought we might do a deal. For a percentage.'

'Depends on the percentage,' I said doubtfully. 'I've never taken a farmed out case before. It would have to be something pretty special.'

'It is, Mr Faraday,' said Cardinal Bishop with just a shade too much eagerness in his tone.

'I thought I could take care of the footwork and the office inquiries while you handled the tough stuff.'

'Sounds like an unfair division of labour to me, Mr Bishop,' I said. 'You'd better start talking. Then we'll see.'

Cardinal Bishop lit a half-smoked cheroot

3

he took out of a battered tobacco tin. He blew out a cloud of poisonous smog and put his spent match in my ashtray.

'That's more like it, Mr Faraday,' he said with another burst of insincerity. He drew on the cheroot once or twice and his gold teeth flashed with enthusiasm.

'I had a call from Alcazar Trucking out at Brentwood two, three days ago,' he said. 'One of their drivers and a truck had gone missing.'

'Hi-jacking?' I said. I took down the trucking company's address on my scratch pad.

Cardinal Bishop shook his head. He ran a finger stained yellow with nicotine across his cropped scalp.

'Naw,' he said with a scowl. 'I already thought of that. According to the sheets the truck was carrying rubble when it went. I checked the guy's address; he boards in a rooming house with two other company drivers on the other side of town.'

'So?' I said. I swivelled in my chair and looked out to where yellow bars of sunshine made a dazzle of the traffic on the boulevard.

'Let me get to it, Mr Faraday,' Bishop went on, still in the same whining tone. 'I been in this game long enough to know what's what.'

'That's why you've come to me?' I said politely.

Bishop studied the end of his cheroot and ignored my remark. 'Anyways,' he went on. 'I sniffed around for a couple of days. I checked

4

up where the truck had been working.'

'What were they doing?' I said.

'Alcazar had a contract for a city housing project,' the fat man said. 'All they were doing was taking the excavated earth and dumping it outside town.'

'They earn big money for that,' I said. 'Shift work. Two drivers falling out?'

Bishop scowled again. 'Maybe, maybe,' he said. 'But somehow I don't think so.'

'What's the name of the client at Alcazar Trucking?' I said. 'The guy who hired you?'

Bishop sighed. 'I didn't get to finish. Davidson owns the company. It was him sent for me.'

I made a note of that too.

'There must be more,' I said. 'Else you wouldn't be here.'

Bishop gave me another eight and a half millimetres of gold filling. 'There is,' he said heavily, 'if you let me get it out. I went over the housing contract site. Nothing. Guy had left the site with a load as usual. He hadn't turned up at the regular tipping place.'

'Perhaps he found a better one.' I said.

Bishop nodded once or twice. 'Bright, Mr Faraday,' he said. 'Bright. My thinking was good. I done right in contacting you, I can see that. I did a bit more footwork, then I gassed up the car and went over the guy's route.'

'You haven't told me his name yet,' I said.

The breath came out of Bishop's mouth like

5

air escaping from a burst balloon.

'Kovacs. Charlie Kovacs. Now can I get on?'

'Sure,' I said. I filled in one or two points on my pad. 'You can cut down on the descriptive.'

Bishop bit on his cheroot so hard it almost broke in two. 'A guy wouldn't find it awful hard to dislike you,' he said.

'I'm only in it for the money,' I said.

'I was up Tintoretto Canyon this morning,' Bishop went on. 'There were tyre-tracks leading off. I found Kovacs' body. Looked like he'd been shot through the head. No sign of the truck.'

He studied his finger-nails and crossed his legs ostentatiously. A fly buzzed loudly in the sudden silence.

'That's interesting,' I said.

'I thought you'd find it so,' said Bishop. His shifty eyes studied me a shade too carelessly.

'You gave the law a call?' I said.

Bishop shook his head. His eyes fixed me with something like supplication in them.

'I can't afford to get mixed up with the law in my business,' he said. 'I beat it straight across to you.'

'Too bad,' I told him. 'Homicide won't like it, Bishop.'

The fat man stubbed out his cheroot in my tray; he looked hopelessly at the pointed toes of his cheap shoes.

'They don't have to know,' he said with a flash of cunning in his already insincere eyes.

6

'Not if you went up there, Faraday, and made the discovery.'

'After you'd already been retained by Davidson,' I said. 'Use your marbles. That wouldn't stand up for five minutes.'

'It might if you said I'd come to you before the body was found,' Bishop said. 'I thought you might do it to help a fellow operative.'

I winced; Bishop tried not to look offended.

'I'll overlook your last remark you overfed little man,' I said. I went over and looked down at the boulevard. I turned to face him. He looked like a bag of jelly sagged in the chair in front of my desk.

'You sure you told me everything?' I said.

'Sure, Mr Faraday,' he said. 'If I swear on my mother's—'

'Don't risk it,' I said. 'Your mother might not like it.'

I went and sat down at my broadtop again. I frowned at Bishop through the thin streamers of smoke that still curled up from the ashtray. 'You told anybody about this at all?'

He shook his head. 'You see, Mr Faraday, I had a little trouble with the cops once before. They threatened to revoke my licence if I got in any more difficulties.'

'I bet they did,' I said. I got out my large-scale map of the L.A. area and studied it, turning over a few facts in my mind. 'You left Kovacs where you found him and came straight back?'

Bishop nodded. 'We could go in my car,' he said. 'It's right outside.'

'That would be sensible,' I said. 'Considering what you've just told me. The police may be there already.'

Bishop looked sheepish. 'I hadn't thought about that,' he admitted. 'This party looks a bit too rough for me. I thought we might split fifty-fifty.'

I gave him a long, hard look.

'Forty-sixty,' he said hastily.

'We'll see,' I said. 'I haven't yet said whether I'm interested or whether you go out that door with the toe of my brogue in the right place.'

'There's no need to get tough, Faraday,' he said in a high, strangled voice.

I ignored him and went on looking at the map. 'I'll see Davidson myself and explain,' I said. 'If I take this thing up. And something tells me I'd be halfway to the psycho ward if I believed more than three-tenths of what you've told me.'

'Believe me, Mr Faraday, if I drop dead right now . . .' he said.

He broke off when he saw the expression on my face. I waited for him to drop dead. It surprised me when I saw him still sitting in the chair.

'I'll have a look up there, Bishop,' I said. 'But I'm not promising anything.'

8

2

I fumigated the office after Bishop left, scrawled a note to Stella and got down to street level. The elevator wasn't working, so I pounded the linoleum; like always, the place smelt of stale carbolic and unredeemed hopes. I walked two blocks to where I'd parked my old powder-blue Buick convertible and slid behind the wheel. On the way across town I checked on the large-scale map of L.A. while killing time in a traffic-jam.

I stopped at Jinty's to get outside their blue-plate special and an iced beer; it wasn't crowded this time of day and it was quiet in the booth. I bought a package of cigarettes at the long bar and came away just before three. Once I got on the freeway I started making mileage. It wasn't a long run and there was a cool breeze which took some of the bite out of the smog. The Buick had just been leathered but I could see fine particles of grit powdering the bonnet like dark snow.

The foothills were high and blue when I tooled the Buick off the highway and on to a secondary metalled road leading upwards round shoulders of green shrub and vegetation. There were some nice houses up on the heights and the ladies who were home from their shopping excursions were showing a fine acreage of tanned flesh on their pool-patios. I jerked my eyes back to the road as a red-head with a 36-18-34 figure scuttled across clean-shaved turf and took a header into a blue-tiled swimpool shaped like a guitar.

It had a bad effect on my driving and I was glad when I left the residential section and struck the fork to Tintoretto; the Buick's wheels made a rough song over the gravelled track and walls of white limestone started throwing back the heat of the sun. The road twisted round hair-pin bends for a bit and then I drew the Buick in on the verge and killed the motor. It was very warm and still up here, with only the long, high, insistent note of a bird that repeated itself every ten seconds or so.

I got out of the car, lit a cigarette and started to walk quietly up, treading softly on the turf at the road-edge. The bird went on practising its scales in the heat and the silence. I stroked out my cigarette with the heel of my shoe. This seemed like the place Bishop had described, a narrow fork that turned off the main canyon drive and spiralled farther up the hillside.

I looked around slowly. There was a house way back off the road, set on stilts, with green wood shutters and a double car-port. It had white entrance gates with a bowed white wood canopy over the top of them, like a Chinese pavilion in an old print. Nothing moved on the green turf or in the flower garden beyond. The water in the pool set in its turquoise tiled surround didn't show a ripple in the stillness which gripped the place.

I got off the road and went up the fork; I could see the tyre-marks of a big truck in the dust of the dirt road. It died out on a stony platform over which the road ran and then went on up the canyon: I walked to the right, down a steeply shelving bank; the grass and dust had been disturbed here. It looked like something or somebody had been dragging a heavy sack down into the ravine bottom. I went down to where Bishop had told me to look. There was nothing in the grass except a heavy impression which might or might not have been caused by a man named Kovacs.

I got down closer; the grass stems were gradually straightening upwards. The sun was very warm here, low on the ground, and I could smell the moist, good smell of earth and damp grass. I put my hand on to the ground and felt the vegetation; there was a patch of something like rust. My forefinger came away sticky and moist. I wiped my fingers on a patch of dry grass and got up thoughtfully.

Something buzzed loudly in the dead silence. A big blowfly with a greeny-blue sheen on its wings came and perched on a twig and glanced at me; it probed delicately with its forefeet at the russet patch, looked at me hesitantly with its many-faceted eyes. The wicked thing buzzed loudly again, as though with alarm, and flew off.

'You and me both,' I said.

I turned to go up the bank behind me. There would be plenty of time to look for the truck.

It was only then I noticed a man's dark shadow stencilled on the white dust at my feet.

Chapter Two

A Long, Cool Drink

1

He was a short, broad-shouldered man, dressed in a light grey suit and soft tan shoes. He wore a lilac shirt and a blue bow tie with white dots seemed like a butterfly hanging under his big chin. A thin rim of sandy hair surrounded his pink bald head like a halo; he had ears that stood out like handles at the side of his face.

He looked mild enough but I wouldn't have made a book on it; there was a bulge under his left arm-pit that could have been made by fat, his wallet or by something else again. And I earned my living by sizing up people's personalities. He was standing at the top of the bank too, right where I would I have to pass him by. I decided to play it easy.

'Looking for something?' he said.

'I might,' I said. 'You never know in my line of business.'

'What would that be?' he asked.

'Dried fruit importer,' I said.

He laughed. 'A dangerous profession.'

'Especially when the prunes start biting back,' I said.

He opened his teeth in silent mirth. 'A sense of humour as well. Capital. Shall we walk?'

'We may as well,' I said. 'Seeing that you're at the top of the bank. Apart from what you've got up your sleeve.'

'Or in my pocket,' he said softly. 'You're sensible.'

I shrugged. I climbed up the bank. He watched me closely. Near to he looked harder than he had seemed from a distance. His suit was stretched across his shoulders in a way that indicated solid muscle. He fell in alongside as we went back towards the road.

'I own the spread up there,' he said, waving his hand. 'I thought you might like to join me for a drink.'

His gesture indicated the house with the swimpool and the Chinese entrance gate.

'And if I don't care for a drink?' I said.

He narrowed his eyes. 'That would be something else again. But you look like a man with a thirst on him. Something long and cool, shall we say?'

He dropped his hand back into his pocket in a way that was so natural and inevitable that it would have deceived nine people out of ten. I was the tenth. He hesitated for the slightest fraction and the air seemed suddenly to have grown close and thundery. Even the birds had stopped singing.

'Why not?' I said.

The short man took his hand out of his pocket again and smiled another non-smile. As an expression of geniality it didn't mean a thing. It was simply his professional manner that was as automatic and reflexive to him as the switching on and off of a bathroom light might be to an ordinary man; part of his stock in trade. I decided to test him out. I walked over to the other side of the road and fell in on his left hand, the side away from where his gun-arm would be; if he had a gun, that is.

He frowned. As we walked up to the gate of his house that looked like something out of a Chinese painting he dropped behind for a moment; when he re-joined me he walked on my left. Again, it was beautifully done, but it still didn't win him a stick of rock so far as I was concerned. We went in under the high bar of the gate and up a drive floored with green stone chippings. They crunched uneasily under our feet. The front of the house looked blank and dead in the stillness of the day and the warmth of the sunlight. There was no-one about. The water lapped softly at the edges of the turquoise tiled swimpool. The green wood shutters were closed over the windows of the

14

top floor and there were dark shadows between the big stilts on which the house was set.

There was a white Dodge sport job parked in one half of the double car port; the car port had cream plastic roofing that reflected back the shimmer of the sun.

He paused as we got up near the car.

'Before we get that drink,' he said, 'I'd be obliged if you'd give me a hand with the car. My staff are away today or I wouldn't have troubled you. I saw you go by and thought you might help.'

He stood there blinking in the sunshine and trying to look genial. He didn't make a very good job of it.

'Sure,' I said. 'What seems to be wrong?'

He led the way in under the plastic roofing; the stench of gasoline came up strong and hot in the confined space.

'Something shorting out under the bonnet,' he said. 'I'm a child at this sort of thing.'

He leaned in under the instrument dash; there was a click and the bonnet of the white Dodge came up sweetly. I watched him closely. He smiled again, licked his lips. I kept my eye on his right-hand pocket.

'I'll have a look-see,' I said. I had a pen-flashlight in my inside pocket and I got it out. The bald man stood aside and I walked around in front of him. I dropped the pen down on to the floor of the car-port. I bent

15

down to pick it up. In the wing mirror of the Dodge I could see jug-ears. He reached down inside the body of the car and came up with a short, blunt-edge fire extinguisher. He whirled it above his head. I could see by the expression of his eyes that he was playing for keeps so I spun aside. The extinguisher came down with a crash on the car wing and a thin stream of foam came hissing out of the nozzle.

He grunted but by this time I had got upright and put my right fist into his belly; to my surprise he was rock-hard here and though he sagged against the car and gave another grunt it didn't stop him. I had the extinguisher arm by then and put the pressure on; saliva dribbled out of the corner of his mouth. The extinguisher twisted in his hand and he screamed as the liquid went into his eyes. He dropped it and whimpered in pain. The extinguisher went on squirting out foam over the cushions of the car. I put an arm-lock on and the sandy-fringed man rocked over the tonneau.

'You chose the wrong man, old dear,' I said softly. I brought the side of my hand down on the bridge of his nose with a crack. His eyes closed and he moaned. He started to go down and I slammed his head against the door panel to finish him off. He hit the concrete with a slap that seemed to rock the car-port and rolled over on his face. The hissing of the extinguisher went on.

16

I went to the side of the house and listened; nothing moved in the garden except the tops of the trees, waving stiffly in the slight breeze. The sound of the birds went on. I went back into the car-port and picked up my pen. I put it back inside my pocket. I found I was breathing a little harder than I thought.

The bald-headed man lay with his face to the concrete. I felt his heart. He was breathing heavily through his nose. I rolled him over so that he could get some air. He looked like he would be out around an hour. I lit a cigarette and studied him carefully. The thin hissing of the extinguisher finally ceased. The foam had made a mess of the Dodge interior. I pinched out the match between my thumb and forefinger and put it back in the box. I searched bald-head; he didn't have a gun after all. The broad-shouldered man lay and breathed heavily at the plastic roofing.

'You try something long and cool, chum,' I said. I went out the car-port, treading softly on the grass and avoiding the gravel. I took the side entrance and went around the building. The place had that empty atmosphere that is quite unmistakeable. We'd made enough row in the car-port to bring half a dozen people on the run if there'd been anybody home.

There was a marble-floored terrace in rear of the building that must have cost more than the rented place I lived in over on Park West. There were one or two statues set on plinths up and down the terrace that looked like the real thing. There were cedarwood French doors that ran the length of the house here. I peered in; there was a library that must have been more than sixty feet long. The books in the shelves looked like they'd been read too; you can always tell when people buy books for show and when they actually read them. This looked like a real bibliophile's lay-out. It didn't tie in with the style of the man lying in the car-port—if he did own the house, like he said.

I frowned. I glanced around the garden; a lawn running to several acres faded out into the far distance; the waters of a lake sparkled behind a high hedge and farther off still, the fretted roof of a Chinese pavilion pricked the sky. I went down the terrace trying the French doors, but they were all locked. I peeked through into several other rooms but there was no-one around.

By now I had toured all the building and I had been away a quarter of an hour by my watch; it was time to get moving. I looked in the car-port as I passed but my friend in the grey suit hadn't stirred from his position. It was a fine afternoon for a quiet sleep. I went back down the drive, my feet crunching loudly in the green gravel and the house sat and watched me from behind the green shutters.

I walked back to the Buick and climbed in. I sat and finished off my cigarette. The wind sighed to itself in the tops of the trees and I wondered why truck-drivers got themselves killed and then disappeared and why well-dressed bibliophiles would want to get murderous with fire-extinguishers. But then I always do have trouble in figuring these things out at the beginning of a case. I began to see why Cardinal Bishop felt it was just a little too much for him to handle.

I put the Buick in gear and tooled slowly down the canyon. The red-haired job was still sunning herself on the pool-patio as I passed. She gave me a lazy wave that disturbed my reasoning all the way back to L.A.

2

Stella leaned over my desk and arched her eyebrows in incredulity. 'Seems like you always get in trouble as soon as my back's turned,' she said. 'Do you mind if I have that again?'

I went through it once more. She grinned suddenly. 'And you just left him lying there?'

'It seemed like a good idea at the time,' I said. I lit a cigarette and walked over to the window and looked down at the boulevard; the traffic went by with a steady hum. Behind the partitioned-off alcove where we brewed the coffee the aroma of freshly-roasted beans came pleasantly to the nostrils. 'Item one,' I said. 'A truck is hi-jacked and the driver murdered. Item two, the truck disappears.'

'Then the body,' put in Stella.

'High marks for originality,' I said. 'Then a joker takes a swing at me. Ten to one he won't be the owner of the house with the green shutters. That wouldn't be very clever.'

Stella ran a delicate finger through her honey-blonde hair and patted it into place. She wore a gold tailored suit that was held in by a black belt; her figure made pleasing undulations underneath it. She saw my glance and smiled; she went on patting her hair, confident in the ability of her profile to hold my attention.

'This Mr Bishop seems a nasty little man from what you say,' she said.

'And then some,' I said. 'His idea of getting tough is a straight three rounds with a chihuahua. And then the dog would win on points.'

Stella actually smiled at that; I went on smoking and looking at nothing in particular out of the window.

'So where does it get us, Mike?' asked Stella.

'Nowhere,' I said. 'Except that the man with the fire extinguisher wasn't there by accident. Odds are that he had something to do with the Kovacs kill.'

'Which means you'll have to look out there again,' Stella said.

I came over and sat down at my desk. Stella went and fussed with cups and saucers and pleasant liquids beyond the screen. I sat and

20

finished my cigarette and waited for the coffee like one of Pavlov's dogs. I guess I was becoming conditioned to Stella's comforts. Which wasn't entirely a good thing. Stella repeated her question. She put my coffee cup down on the blotter, fetched her own and sat down opposite.

'I guess so,' I said. 'A look up the canyon seems to be indicated. Jug-ears may have had something to do with removing the body. He could have found the empty house and parked his car in the port and pretended to be the owner.'

Stella cupped her hands round the coffee beaker and sipped thoughtfully.

'My, we are a clever boy today,' she said approvingly.

'It's all this sunlight,' I said modestly. 'Keeps the brain cells circulating.'

'Or Archdeacon Pope or whatever he calls himself might be the biggest liar in Christendom,' she said softly.

'The thought had crossed my mind,' I said. I sipped at the black liquid in my cup. It grinned back up at me. Just then the phone buzzed.

Stella's body uncoiled out of her chair with a rustle and she languidly scooped up the phone from its cradle. Her eyes sparkled with mischief as she handed it over to me.

'The man himself,' she said. She went back over to her own desk and picked up the extension, turned over her scratchpad.

21

'Bishop here,' said the voice.

I sighed and settled back in my chair.

'The answer is no,' I said. 'What's the question?'

Bishop's voice, heavy with resignation and years of insult came over the wire. 'Just wondered how you were making out.'

'So-so,' I said. 'Nothing to report really. No body there. And some party with jug-ears and a natty line in suiting tried to part my hair with a fire-extinguisher.'

Bishop's breath went out in a loud puff at the other end and there was a long silence. I could feel his fright way off from where he was phoning.

'Looks like I done right to come to you,' he said at last.

'You might say that,' I admitted. 'But the wear and tear will come out of your slice.'

I heard a choking sound coming from the instrument; I held it away from my ear. Stella smiled at me, her hand over the mouthpiece of her own phone. When Bishop had recovered he started to make rather a lot of noise.

'What's your next move?' he asked when he had calmed down.

'I'll decide that,' I told him. 'You just keep your fat hide out of trouble and go on about your rent-collecting.'

'Well, I'll be in touch, Mr Faraday,' he said gloomily.

'You do that,' I said and slammed the phone

down. Stella smiled again. She listened at her phone for a while longer and then put it back on its plastic cradle.

'There doesn't seem to be a very great bond of affection between you and Mr Bishop,' she said.

'You haven't met him,' I told her.

She was still smiling when I closed the door behind me.

Chapter Three

Man With a Tin Leg

1

The head office of Alcazar Trucking was on one of the main stems on the other side of town. It was an impressive lay-out. I sent in my card to Davidson via a blonde job with tip-tilted breasts that were difficult to avoid looking at. She was dressed in a blue candy-striped blouse that strained against whatever she'd got underneath and her blue skirt that looked like it had been painted on her bare skin was vibrating at 68 r.p.m., as she walked down the hall away from me. Front or back it was a pleasure or an ordeal, whichever way you looked at it.

Speaking for myself I can take that sort of

stuff all day. She came back soon after and gave me a chance to study the front view.

'I'm sorry, Mr Faraday. Mr Davidson's down in the yard supervising loading operations. If you'd like to wait . . .'

'It's no bother,' I said. 'I'll go down and see him if it's all the same to you.'

'Surely,' she said. 'You can see the bay from this window.'

I looked across from the office-block to where row after row of steel-girdered roofs rose on concrete piers. On the tarmac aprons in front, ranks of big Chevvy trucks stood waiting; the air was heavy with the low thunder of their engines and the distinctive smell of diesel fuel came up hot and acrid through the open window.

'How will I know him?' I asked.

The blonde job smiled slightly. 'You'll know him, Mr Faraday. He's only got one leg.'

I nodded, gave her one of my Grade A smiles and went on out. I walked down a broad staircase walled in bleached natural wood panelling and through an entrance hall full of girl typists, whose efforts sounded like a colony of woodpeckers having a field day. I got down the granite steps flanking the glass-fronted block and struck out across the tarmac. If I thought I was looking for some sort of cripple I soon revised my thinking. I spotted Davidson some way off; he was about eight feet tall and proportionately broad. He was swearing at a

24

truck driver and walking rapidly down the bays at the same time; I noticed he had a limp but that was all. The truckie was having to run to keep up with him.

When I caught up he was just finishing blasting the driver out. The other was a big man too, with sandy hair, but when Davidson had finished with him he looked white around the gills, and about two feet tall. If Davidson had gone on I figured he would soon have bust out crying.

'Yes, sir,' he said when Davidson gave him a slot in the monologue and scuttled back towards his cab.

Davidson turned a couple of steel-grey eyes on me. 'What can I do for you?' he said curtly. He wasn't impolite but there was frost on the syllables as thick as cake-icing. I handed him the photostat of my licence in the plastic holder. He studied it for a moment with eyes that looked like hoods had come down over them.

'Another one, eh?' he said gently. He passed me the folder back. 'I figured Bishop wasn't man enough for the job. You figure you're big enough, Mr Faraday?'

'We'll see,' I said easily. 'A boy's a boy and a man's a man and Bishop's neither.'

He relaxed a little but his voice was just as frosty. 'I'm not paying two fees just to have you trace a missing truck,' he said.

'Did I say anything about money?' I asked.

25

He scuffed the tarmac with the toe of a tan leather riding boot.

'Well, maybe I was a little sharp off the mark,' he admitted. 'Everyone puts the bite on me for something around here.'

I said nothing but waited for him to go on.

'We'd better go in the office,' he said. 'We can talk better in there.'

He caught me looking down at his leg. There was an identical brown boot on each foot so I guessed he was wearing one of the fancy tin sort.

'Okinawa,' he said softly. 'But don't waste your sympathy. You'll find I can keep up all right.'

'Sure,' I said. 'I just wondered why your secretary had to mention it at all.'

He grinned suddenly. It looked good on his big, ugly face. 'She's got a mother complex,' he said. 'She tries to spare me all the footwork.'

He gave me a sharp but not unfriendly look.

'She tries too hard,' he said. He started walking back towards the office block. I fell in beside him. He turned and waved his hand in the air. The yard was filled with the heavy throb of motors as the drivers revved up. The big jobs started lumbering out of the yard. We stood and watched them. Davidson stared into the far distance as the last disappeared out of the gate. There must have been more than fifty all told and more parked in the bays. 'Shows where hard work can get you,'

Davidson said. 'Started in 1946 with just one broken-down ex-Army job.'

He led the way in through the vestibule and up the stairs; his limp was more noticeable on the up-grade and he had to cling on to the handrail and haul himself up, step by step. I could see sweat glistening suddenly in the roots of his thick hair. We went in over the heavy grey carpet towards his office. It was a big, cream painted room with green Venetian blinds and two heavy teak desks littered with docket forms, ashtrays and yellow telephones. Davidson nodded me into a brown plastic high-backed chair tarted up to look like leather. I noticed his own chair was the real thing.

He sat down opposite me and flipped over a packet of cigarettes. I lit up and passed the pack back to him.

'Just where do you fit in, Mr Faraday?' he asked. He pressed a button on his desk.

'I'm not to be disturbed for the next thirty minutes, Miss Kringle,' he spat into the intercom. He flipped off the switch and turned to face me. I put my spent match into a black onyx ashtray that had a silver model of a truck let into one side of it.

'Nowhere at the moment,' I said. 'The thing just interests me, that's all. And someone tried to part my hair with a fire-extinguisher. Someone who might know something about your truck—and the driver.'

Davidson's eyes were suddenly hot and hard

and full of lights. 'The hell he did,' he said. He waited for me to go on. I didn't tell him about Kovacs; it wouldn't have done any good at that stage.

'I'd like carte blanche to nose around your outfit,' I said. 'I want to question the drivers, perhaps take a trip on the same route Kovacs took.'

'Take it as read,' Davidson said. He scribbled something on a sheet of headed notepaper he took out of one of his desk drawers. He signed with a flourish and flipped it over to me. 'Here's your authorization, Mr Faraday.'

I picked up the sheet without looking at it and put it in my pocket.

'We'd better have a run-down on the business, the routes and so forth,' I said. 'I'll get to that in a minute. I'd like to know something about Kovacs, his record, stuff like that. I gather the truck was empty.'

Davidson nodded. 'Cost me nearly thirty thousand dollars, though. New type. First of three being delivered. Biggest truck I had. That mean anything to you?'

'It might,' I said, 'and then again it might not. You were insured, of course?'

Davidson nodded again. He looked chunky and big and as tough as one of his own trucks, sitting firm and solid in the leather chair.

'That's hardly the point, Mr Faraday,' he said with surprising mildness.

28

'I agree,' I told him, 'but there's a number of angles to this. For instance, the weight and load; would that affect the number of trips in a given period?'

'Bound to,' said Davidson. 'Biggest truck, longer to load and turn around; slower and more dangerous to handle at speed. On the other hand they carry nearly three times the normal capacity.'

'Of earth,' I said.

'Meaning what?' Davidson asked.

'The time factor,' I said. 'Kovacs was paid by the trip, I take it?'

Davidson's eyes were suddenly hard again. 'Go on,' he said stiffly.

'The longer the journey and the turn-round, the less pay,' I said. 'You see what I'm getting at.'

Davidson's eyes smouldered. 'He was taking short-cuts by dumping the earth in an unauthorized location,' he said heatedly.

'He could have been,' I said. 'I've got no proof of that for now. But at least the facts fit.'

Davidson drummed his big hand on the top of his desk; his brow corrugated with thought.

'Keep me informed, Mr Faraday,' he said. 'In the meantime I'll get the information you want from Miss Kringle. I'll have someone drop by your office some time this afternoon with the stuff. You got an office, of course?'

'No, I operate from a cracker barrel on the edge of town,' I told him. 'The one near the swamp on the other side of the rail yards.'

Davidson flushed and then grinned. 'I asked for that one, Mr Faraday,' he said. 'I'm used to dealing with people like Bishop.'

'That's all right,' I said. 'So long as we know where we stand. I may be around tomorrow.'

I stood up and passed over to him one of my printed cards. He studied it, holding it delicately for a man with such big hands.

'Yeah, sure,' he said. 'That stuff will be over by seven at the latest.'

It felt like my fingers were going through a meat-grinder when we shook hands.

'I'll be in touch,' I said.

I went out, threaded my way between the woodpeckers, got in my Buick and drove off.

Chapter Four

Near-Miss

1

I got outside a sandwich and a tall glass of Pabst at a downtown bar and then drove on over to my rented place on Park West. I ran a quick shower. While I was dressing, the phone rang. It was Stella to say the stuff had turned up from Davidson like he'd promised. I gave him a high rating for efficiency. Stella said there was nothing special in the information; nothing that stuck out, at any rate. I thanked her for hanging on and told her I'd be in in the morning.

I went up to my bedroom and checked on the armoury I kept in a locked cupboard. I broke out the Smith Wesson, put it in the webbing shoulder holster, together with a spare clip. Usually, a private investigator gets about one case in ten where there's real trouble; this promised to be one of them.

It was just turned eight when I drove across town again and it wouldn't be properly dark for the best part of two hours. Plenty of time for what I wanted to do. I drove up Tintoretto Canyon and stopped the Buick about a mile from the house with the green shutters; I found a layby cut out of the solid shoulder of rock, with a thin screen of trees between it and the highway. There were no other cars parked there and sparse traffic on the road. I got out the car and picked up the leather case I'd brought out with me; the sun was still hot and stung astringently throught my thin suit and across my shoulders as I went down the concrete strip.

Presently I found what I was looking for, a spidery trackway that zig-zagged up the hard rock face of the shoulder, between spiky clumps of evergreen trees. I was in a lather of sweat before I'd gone halfway up the slope and stopped to take off my jacket; I rolled it up, with the Smith-Wesson holster inside it and tucked it under my arm. The case containing the binoculars bumped awkwardly against my hips as I made diagonal tracks up through the stifling heat of the underbrush.

I stopped again at a bend in the pathway and rolled up my shirtsleeves; I could see only the sky between the tops of the trees, it was so dense in here, but the shadows were beginning to etch themselves more lengthily on the ground. After another five minutes' hard going I came out on a rocky plateau and took a brief fix by the sun. If my orientation was right the place I was aiming for should be about a mile and a half off, and I wanted to avoid the big private estates and particularly the house owned by the bald-headed man who liked to sleep on his garage floor in the afternoons.

I struck out in what seemed the most likely direction and in a few minutes was going downhill again, keeping my bearings by the sun. The going was easier here and I made good time. I could hear the distant roar of traffic from the highway after another half mile. I was walking through scrub with rock and sandy outcrops underfoot but the sun hadn't lost much of its heat.

I transferred the binoculars to my free left hand and shortened the straps so that they wouldn't bump against the ground; the terrain started going uphill again and another few minutes brought me to a narrow plateau, fringed with trees on one side. I could see the sparkle of a lake in the distance and figured it might be the house with the green shutters. I got out the glasses and confirmed that it was; the detail of the house beyond the ornamental trees stood out with startling clarity but nothing moved on the terrace.

I put back the binoculars in the case and pushed on. I now had my position and it was a comparatively simple operation to pinpoint the spot where Bishop said the truck-driver's body had been lying. I was passing some hundred yards to the east of it, of course, on private ground; what I was looking for now was a high vantage point which would enable me to see some way up the dirt road farther along Tintoretto Canyon. The place I would have looked at if jug-ears hadn't interrupted me.

I had just got into thick cover a little down the slope when I heard the beat of a motor coming up behind me; it had the distinctive chopping sound of a helicopter rotor and I got in under a bush and looked over my shoulder. There was a big, grey-painted machine cruising up low over the ground as though looking for something; I got in farther under the bush and remained still. The buzzing of insects in the dying heat of the day sounded loud even against the helicopter's efforts.

There appeared to be two men in the cabin blister; the machine went up and down two or three times, hesitantly, like it was engaged in a box search. Then it rose almost vertically and went off due north. I waited until it was a faint speck above the horizon and then came out of hiding. It was a little cooler now and I put my holster back on and my coat over it. I went on down the slight slope and when I looked through a screen of brush I found I could see a U-bend of the dirt road.

This was about half a mile farther up than I'd gone that afternoon. I got out the binoculars, settled myself behind a low rock and focussed up. I raked the country in a slow arc, starting in the west and going east until the eyepiece blurred with the fuzzy green of the nearer foliage on the hillside in front of me. The Zeiss coated lenses were lovely jobs; I could see every detail, every blade of grass in the glowing warmth of the late evening sunshine. Thank you, Bill Wordsworth, I said to myself.

I twirled the focussing screw and worked my way up the U-strip of road in front of me from south to north. I soon came on a high wire fence strung across the road. It had a white five-bar gate set in it and each side of the fence two big notice boards stapled to the wire; they proclaimed in red letters; STRICTLY PRIVATE—NO ADMITTANCE —KEEP OUT. A fairly straightforward exhortation. I heard the sound of a motor then and took the glasses down from my eyes. It wasn't the helicopter coming back, as I had expected. I saw the white blur of a car bonnet coming out of the trees from somewhere underneath me; the machine drifted round the bend pretty fast and then feathered to a stop in the thick dust in front of the five-bar gate. I worked the focussing screw again and the bodywork of the white Dodge sport job I'd last seen in the car-port of the house with the green shutters stroked into sharp-edged relief. Or at least one very like it. There was a stocky man with salt and pepper hair sitting at the wheel of the car; he had his back to me, naturally, so I didn't get to see his face.

His companion was a different proposition altogether; she was a natural blonde if I could trust Zeiss of Jena. And somehow I felt I could. She stood and fiddled with a key in a padlock on the gate while the stocky man drummed his hands impatiently on the rim of the steering wheel. The girl got the padlock unfixed in the end and got the gate open; I couldn't see her face properly as she stood beyond the end of the gate while the stocky man drove through. She wore a green two-piece of some light material and she moved like a gazelle.

I switched from her back to the white sport job. I was hoping the driver was going to turn around but he just sat immobile while he waited for the girl to lock the gate again. When I swung back to her she'd already done that and was walking away from me. She got in beside the driver and they drove off up the road in a plume of dust. I moved the binoculars ahead of them, following the long curve of the road in the evening light, re-focussing as I went. I didn't know what I was looking for. Whatever it was didn't bear any resemblance to what I eventually saw.

I stopped on a blur of huts and fencing posts, swung back. By the time I had the scene clear the white Dodge had pulled into the picture again and stopped. In the background were dark trees and hills and the road wound into them. Across the road was another high fence of wire with notices. Electric lamps were carried on the tops of high metal poles like you sometimes see on the Continent of Europe. Thick cables were slung between them. Combined with the high wire fence it looked something like a concentration camp.

A stark black sign at the roadside said: HALT. Across the road were strung two big striped poles with netting which reached down to the ground. The poles had heavy counterweights on them and a wheeled handle at each side. Two men in dark grey uniforms stood behind the striped poles and signalled to the people in the car. They had sub-machine guns cradled in their arms. The girl and the man got out and came up towards the barrier.

Two other men in black started turning the wheels and the striped metal barriers came up towards the sky. The two armed men and the man and the girl went into a hut which was set back from the road inside the wire. I was left staring stupidly at a board which said in black on white: DOUANE: CUSTOMS—ALL PASSPORTS TO BE SHOWN.

'What the hell?' I said out loud. I was about to put down the glasses when there came a loud crack in the sleepy silence of the hillside. Something struck the rock near my head with frightening force, making a loud, dead whine and splinters of stone flew as a dull white scar spread in front of my eyes.

2

I went down the hillside in a long, slithering dive that was more fright and instinct than professional skill; the hot-ice which seared my spine was already giving way to a self-disgust at my lack of professionalism. I had been so busy watching a customs post that might so easily have been a typical Hollywood film set, I had completely forgotten that I myself could just as easily be under observation. I was already yanking at the Smith-Wesson as I rolled but no further shot followed; I fetched up against the solid trunk of a pine tree and got the other side of it in no-seconds flat. I found I was sweating and the breath was coming out of my nostrils with a noise which had me worried. That the action was unexpected was no excuse.

I put an eye slowly round the trunk, lazily

raked the hillside; there was a group of tall trees at the top which might conceal the sniper. It had seemed to me that the shot had come from the left and above from the angle it appeared to chip the rock. I remembered the helicopter then; they would have reported my movements on the slope quite a while ago, may well have had me in their own field-glasses before I noted their motor.

I listened for a long minute but there was nothing suspicious; no-one moved and the only sound was the sharp, insistent hammer of some bird from way off down the hillside. I found I still had the binoculars in my left hand; I must have trailed them down the slope by the strap. I found they were unbroken. I crouched behind the tree and put them back in their case.

I put my head up once more and listened again. There didn't seem to be any future in hanging around so I slid down the hill backwards, fanning the Smith-Wesson in front of me, until the undergrowth hid the ridge. Then I got the hell out and started putting air between me and the plateau until I was back down near the road. I was feeling pretty mad then and not all at myself; some of it rubbed off on the house with the green shutters. I looked at my watch, made a quick calculation. I sat down behind a tree, put the Smith-Wesson away, lit up a cigarette and started to wait until dark.

An hour passed, getting on for two; I smoked my fifth cigarette. It was almost completely dark when I got up to go and even the birds were silent. A twig crackled under my foot with a sound as loud as a pistol shot. I had the Smith-Wesson out before I realised it was too dark to see anything in this light. And in any case the thick cover would have made shooting impossible, either for myself or anyone who might have followed me.

I bared my teeth in a wry grimace. You're getting old, Faraday, I told myself. I put the revolver back in my shoulder holster and walked down to the road with no attempt at concealment. I could see the lights of passing cars on the highway long before I got to the track. There was nothing in the layby except my Buick. I stopped on my way through and put the binoculars in the dash cubby and locked it.

I looked at myself in the wing mirror; I looked good and dishevelled. I brushed myself down and made myself a little more presentable. There was a long smear of dust on my jacket from where I'd gone down the hillside. I cleaned it off with my handkerchief. I figured I looked respectable enough to get in the average flophouse without causing too much comment.

I went back up to the highway and walked along. Presently lights came up from the side of the road; I went in under the familiar Chinese gateway and up the drive with the green gravel chippings. The Dodge was parked in front of the main entrance. I went up the steps and pressed the bell-nipple set in the white wood upright. Light blinked from an iron lantern set over the top of the door.

A girl stood looking at me in the light of the porch. I'd already seen her before that day. She had long blonde hair and the same green two-piece suit. She looked even better from the front than the back. She looked at me with approval; a faint perfume came from her that reminded me of something.

'Hullo,' she said in one of those voices that make you feel like someone's finger is tickling the base of your spine.

'I'm April Dawn.'

Chapter Five

April Dawn

1

'Are you the one that comes up like thunder?' I asked. 'You know, the one Kipling wrote about.'

She gurgled with pleasure. 'Well, well,' she said. 'Come on in.'

'Thanks,' I said. She stood aside for me to pass her into the hall and once again I caught that elusive perfume. It smelled the way dry grass smells in high summer in the South of France when you're about twenty-five and with the right girl. Except that I was thirty-three and beat up and a private cop in L.A., and with the wrong girl and getting in with the wrong sort of company. Otherwise it was swell, like I said.

'Had an accident with your car?' I said. 'I see there's a dent in the bonnet.'

She shrugged. 'Just a scratch,' she said softly. 'I didn't catch your name.'

'I didn't give it,' I said. 'But just for the record it's Mike Faraday.'

She shook hands gravely. 'Have a drink,' she said. 'Then we'll talk.'

She led the way across a marble-tiled hall through into a big room that marched alongside the windows overlooking the terrace; the walls were dead white, there were white rugs on the floor and most of the chairs and divans were in white leather. Acrid yellow curtains at the windows broke the monotony and made the room come alive; pale yellow shaded lamps formed pools of light that were easy on the eyes.

'What sort of weed-killer do you prefer?' she asked, crossing to a metal cart with a

41

striped awning; it had metal compartments which held just above every type of bottle obtainable. It looked more like a liquor store than a private sideboard.

'Scotch if you've got it,' I said. 'Who's the dipso?'

She smiled. 'We like to keep a little light refreshment in the house, Mr Faraday.'

There was no answer to that so I studied the dark sky out the window while she poured the drink. A glass screen at the end of the room slid back and a Japanese houseboy with slicked black hair and a white coat came in. He walked so quietly on the white rug it looked like he was on castors.

'I can manage, thank you, Hito,' said the girl. Her voice had changed. It cracked like a whip-lash. The Japanese stopped in mid-stride, bowed and melted away through the door through which we'd come in.

'Do sit down, Mr Faraday,' the girl said. She handed me the glass. We clinked rims. She led the way over near where the fireplace would have been if they'd had one. Instead, a sculptor's nightmare that looked like a convoluted ear leaned out of the wall; it was made of white metal and was, I presumed, meant to carry off the smoke from the horizontal steel plate that served as a hearth.

The girl sat on a white silk ottoman and folded her legs under her with a soft shirring of stockings; that was the gambit that was supposed to make my blood race faster. It never failed too.

'What's your trouble, Mr Faraday?' she said.

'No trouble, Miss Dawn,' I said. 'I'm just looking for a gentleman who wears bow ties and lightweight suits. We had a little argument outside your front door this afternoon.'

The girl wrinkled up her brows in a very good imitation of a frown; like she didn't know what I was talking about. I didn't buy it.

'No-one like that lives here,' she said. 'There's only myself and my uncle.'

'A bald-headed character,' I said.

The girl smiled; she put a very pink tongue in her glass and tasted her drink the way an insect tests things with its antennae. Except that she was the very nicest sort of insect; a butterfly perhaps. Her hair shimmered in the lamplight as she shook her head.

'Definitely not uncle,' she said decisively. 'He doesn't like violence, Mr Faraday.'

'Who does, Miss Dawn?' I said guardedly. I put back another half inch of Scotch and leaned forward in my armchair. I sighed. 'Well, I figured he wouldn't live here,' I said. 'But I had to make sure.'

She looked at me steadily over the rim of her glass. 'You wouldn't care to tell me all about it?'

It was my turn to shake my head. 'Not really,' I said. 'But I'd be glad to take up other subjects with you any time. I'm in the book.'

She smiled again. It looked good on her. 'My, we are getting bold,' she said.

'It's the whisky,' I said modestly.

Just when the dialogue was at this interesting stage the glass door slid back again and another man came in; my impatience must have shown on my face for he gave a dry cough before he advanced into the lamplight. It was the bird with the salt-and-pepper hair I'd seen driving up to the customs post with the girl earlier that day. Before, I hadn't been sure but that clinched it; he was unmistakeable, even though I'd only seen him from the back.

'Won't you introduce me to your friend, my dear,' he said easily, in one of those voices that sound like someone walking on tiptoe on broken glass.

'I'm sorry, Jack,' the girl said. We both got up.

'Professor Hilton, this is Mike Faraday,' the girl said. 'He's up here seeing the sights.'

The Professor had a hand like a warm doughnut. 'Pleased to know you, Mr Faraday,' he said with obvious insincerity. 'You won't find much to interest you up here.'

'The sights are fine,' I said, giving April Dawn a glance of approval. She sat down on the divan again grinning. The Professor coughed.

'Well, yes, Mr Faraday, you're a good deal younger than me,' he said. 'Would you care to make me a drink, my dear? The usual.'

He went over and sat on the ottoman facing me as the girl walked back to the drink cart. He studied me from under salt-and-pepper eyebrows. I should have put him at about fifty-five. He wasn't a bad-looking character if you can forget about weak mouths and insincere eyes.

'What are you a professor of, Professor?' I said. 'Or shouldn't I ask?'

He laughed shortly. 'It's no secret, Mr Faraday. Advanced physics is my line. I had a seminar at Berkeley until a couple of years ago. Now I'm in an advisory capacity. Industry and so forth.'

'That's nice,' I said.

'And you?' he asked, raising his eyebrows. He took the glass the girl handed him without looking. She smoothed her skirt and sat down next to him with her legs crossed. She didn't look directly at me but I could feel her eyes didn't leave my face.

'We're in similar fields,' I said.

'Really?' He arched his eyebrows again.

'I investigate various phenomena,' I went on. 'Aberrant behaviour patterns, that sort of thing.'

'Really?' the Professor repeated himself. He drank nervously. 'What specific area?'

'Human nature,' I said.

The Professor seemed to knock back his drink at an amazing rate. I noticed his glass was nearly empty already.

45

'We must get together some time, Mr Faraday,' he said. 'I should imagine we would have a lot in common.'

'Except that the laws of physics run on recognized tram-lines,' I said.

He smiled. 'Whereas human nature . . . Quite. I get your point, Mr Faraday.'

'I thought you would, Prof,' I said.

The girl said nothing. The man with salt-and-pepper hair shifted uneasily on the ottoman. His eyes stared at the girl in mute appeal. She got up with barely-concealed impatience and went back over to the drink-cart.

'What really brought you here, Mr Faraday?' he said, baring his teeth. In anyone else the effect would have been pleasing but on him it looked like a hyaena welcoming its breakfast; the smile was like an insult to his face. Which wasn't saying much.

'We already went over it,' I said. 'Miss Dawn will tell you.'

The smile left his face and fell with a thud on the carpet. He stood up. The girl re-appeared and put the glass in his hand. He drained it at one gulp without looking at either of us.

'In that case, Mr Faraday, don't let me detain you,' he said. 'I have much to do.'

'Sure,' I said. 'Be seeing you.' I sat down again and the girl followed suit. The Professor took one step forward; he glared at both of us.

His mouth worked once or twice, noiselessly, and then he went out, walking like he was on raw egg-yolks.

'Good evening,' he said in a strangled voice as he got to the door. It slid to after him.

The girl laughed. 'Where were we?' she said.

2

I finished my third drink. It was quite dark outside the windows now, only the tips of the nearer trees visible against the blackness.

April Dawn leaned back against the white silk of the divan and studied me from under half-closed lids.

'You mustn't mind my uncle, Mr Faraday,' she said.

'I don't,' I told her. 'I haven't given him another thought all evening.'

She smiled. 'Incidentally, why did you come up here?'

'Just curiosity,' I said.

She finished her own drink off, made as though to say something and then thought better of it. Her eyes were enigmatic in the semi-gloom. I stood up.

'It's been great,' I said.

She stood up too. 'Come again,' April Dawn said. 'You know where we live.'

'I'll do that,' I said. She walked me to the door. In the hall she came up close to me. Her lips brushed mine fleetingly in the brief interval before she passed me and opened the door.

'Don't forget,' she breathed in my ear.

'I'm hardly likely to,' I told her as I tried to stop my motor from rocketing.

She held out her hand formally as we stood framed in the open doorway.

'Goodbye, Mr Faraday,' she said.

I became aware that Professor Hilton was standing at the other end of the hallway watching us. He didn't say anything, just leaned against the wall in silence.

'Goodnight, Miss Dawn,' I said. I stepped out into the darkness and the porch door clicked shut behind me. I went down over the gravel for the second or third time in my life and out under the Chinese archway not sure whether I'd found what I was looking for or whether to slant the set-up another way. True or false April Dawn would be worth another visit.

The traffic was heavier on the highway now and I sprinted across to face into the headlights as I walked. I got back to the layby without being killed and breathed in the heavy scent of the pinewoods. The traffic went by in long, shuddering waves, muffled at this distance from the road, the head and tail lights like attenuated glow worms in the dark. The chirping of crickets from the woods beyond came heavy and urgent to my ear as I went up the layby to the Buick. There were no other cars around. I got in, started the motor, switched on the main beam and edged out on to the road.

I got into the main stream and started making time back to L.A. I lit a cigarette with one hand and smoked as I drove. I went round a curve rather fast and began to drift; I put both hands back on the wheel and over-corrected. I felt a pressure on my shoulder. Something soft and bulky sagged against me. My offside wheels fought the edge of the road and the Buick momentarily scrabbled through scree as I looked to see what it was.

I corrected again as sweat trickled down my face. The glazed eyes of the bald-headed man in the lightweight suit stared into mine as he lolled in the passenger seat. His shirt-front was a mass of clotted carmine. Blood seeping from his mouth, his nostrils and the corners of his eyes made a bizarre mask of his face in the lights from the oncoming cars.

Just to complete my pleasure I heard the thin, high wail of a police siren coming up the canyon road behind me.

Chapter Six

Dead Freight

1

I had perhaps thirty seconds. The white gravel of a roadside track loomed ahead of me. I switched off the car lights and spun the wheel, all in one movement. The car lurched madly, tore round in a screaming U, white dust billowing over the bonnet. I saw the road spin in the rear mirror just before a light blossomed far off down the highway. I trod on the brake; the Buick shuddered and shale and gravel shot like machine-gun bullets from under the wheels.

The car rolled violently, the springs protesting, but I was squarely on the track, the black shadows of saplings whirling by at the track edge frighteningly fast. I spun the wheel again, trying to keep her away from the trees, while I used the brake, bringing her to a more controllable speed without going off the edge. The dead man on the seat next me spun away with the Buick's gyrations; his head struck the windscreen upright with a dull crack.

Dust covered the whole of the windshield, making it difficult to see the faint whiteness of the track shimmering in the moonlight but I daren't use the lights; I hoped there were no tree stumps. Rubber squealed under the car as the brakes began to bite again and then the Buick was stopping, rolling slower, still right side up, still clear of the trees. I found my face drenched with sweat. The track was no longer spinning in front of me. We stopped. I reached with a not quite steady hand and switched off the ignition. The intrusion of a motor into the deep silence was like sacrilege.

The noise of the siren seemed to fill the whole night. I sat and looked in the rear mirror; a big motor cycle went tearing down the highway, the powerful headlight silhouetting the screen of dark trees at the road-edge. The patrolman must have had her up to almost 100 m.p.h. The siren died away and the night was filled with the chatter of the crickets. If I had been just five seconds later I should have been in serious trouble.

When the traffic on the freeway had settled down to normality I reached for my pack of cigarettes and lit up; I sat and smoked, oblivious of the bald-headed man who sat quietly enough and gazed up at the sky. He seemed particularly interested in the star patterns. When I'd finished the cigarette I got out the Buick and went over her as best I could in the moonlight. She was still dead centre of the track and as far as I could see, undamaged; there was only a scrape across the rear offside wing, probably caused by a tree branch. None of the tyres had burst.

I went up the track a way; the crickets stopped their song at the faint vibration of my feet. They seemed to be listening for something. When I stopped on the track they started up again. Presently I found a place that would do; a steep declivity that descended about fifty feet into deep brush. The stone outcroppings of the slope wouldn't leave any traces.

It was very quiet here; I walked on the track verge, in deep shadow and scouted back to the edge of the road. I went round and scuffed over the deep tyre-tracks in the dust I had made going in. Cars hummed by at inter-planetary speeds but the patrolman didn't come back and there was nothing parked nearby. When I judged it was safe I got back in the driving seat of the Buick. I waited until the traffic noises were heaviest and then started my motor. I tooled the Buick down the track at walking speed, still careful not to use my lights.

When I got to the place I had chosen I switched off the motor again. I got my pencil flash and very quickly went over bald-head's pockets. He'd been absolutely cleaned out, as I figured. There wasn't a mark of identification on him. The only thing in his inside jacket pocket was an expensive crocodile skin wallet; this had no identification either. It contained ten single dollar bills.

I put the money and the wallet back as I'd

found it; I sat thinking. I shone the flash on his front. There were five or six wounds, bunched quite close together, in the front of the chest, made by heavy bullets; looked like a burst from a tommy-gun at short range. I opened the passenger door when I'd finished and lugged him out. I wondered if someone had paid him out for his failure to quieten me in the garage at April Dawn's house.

I dragged him along the track and pushed him over. The body went down with a minimum of fuss, falling swiftly, almost clear of the rock, the ground was so steep. He disappeared into the brush and I could hear the crackling for quite some while after as he bored his way deep into the centre. So far as I could see there were no marks on the rock, certainly no bloodstains; the wounds were too old for that. I got a tree branch and dusted along the track for a bit, obliterating the scuff-marks made by his heels.

Then I went over the Buick with the flash, looking for bloodstains on the upholstery. I could see none, but I got a cloth from the dash-cubby anyway and dusted down the front seat; I also wiped the windscreen upright he'd banged against when we'd gone off the road. By the time I'd finished, more than an hour had gone by. I switched on the engine and reversed quickly back to the road. I had to wait ten minutes before I could reverse out without being spotted by cars coming from either direction. Then I put on my main beam and started burning up the miles.

2

I'd been travelling for about five or ten minutes, keeping a sharp eye open, when I saw a light in my mirror; I checked out. I'd seen a police motor-cycle patrolman stationed on the verge at the intersection of a side road about a quarter of a mile farther back. I only had a quick flash of him but he was using his radio telephone. I waited a moment more to make sure and then flicked my headlights for him to overtake. He stayed where he was and I heard the wail of his siren. Looked like he'd been checking on my registration number.

I slowed down and pulled over as he went around me. I stopped the Buick and killed the motor. He drew up a few yards ahead, pushed his big machine up on its support and came back over, getting his notebook out of a front pocket in his black leather slicker. He was a big fellow and I noticed he kept his right hand on the walnut butt of the revolver which protruded from the canvas holster on his hip. I wound down the driving window as he signalled.

'Some trouble, officer?' I said pleasantly, in my Sunday-driver voice. The one I reserved for lady motorists and big traffic cops with short tempers and long reaches. This one had a broad, bony face with a tough jaw below square teeth. His lips were puckered as though he'd been driving at high speed in the teeth of a gale and his green-tinted night-goggles made him look like something out of the War of the Worlds. He pushed the glasses up over the peak of his cap.

He said nothing but came up close to the car and looked in the window. I kept my hands quietly on the wheel and waited for his move. He put a flashlight on my face, then studied his notebook. He looked back at me sharply.

'Mr Faraday, isn't it?' he said in a puzzled voice. He took the flash off my face. I recognized him as a traffic cop called O'Rourke whom I'd once or twice had dealings with. I was glad I'd bought tickets for the Police Orphans Benefit.

'You look like somebody cheated you out of an arrest,' I said.

The big cop grinned. He switched off the flashlight and took his other hand away from his belt.

'You wouldn't have a corpse in there by any chance?' he said laconically.

'Help yourself,' I said. He put the flashlight across the open seats of the convertible in a bored manner. I hoped my casual smile didn't look too lop-sided.

He consulted his notebook again. 'Sure got your number right, though,' he said, the puzzlement back in his voice. He made a note in the book with a blue and silver pencil he took out of the leather loop on top of the notebook. He looked at his wrist-watch and added the time.

'Just hold on, Mr Faraday,' he said. 'It won't take a minute to straighten this out.'

He went back to his motor-cycle and I saw him lift his phone. I sat and studied the night foliage at the side of the road and hoped the lights of passing cars wouldn't give my face away. I saw O'Rourke look curiously back in my direction once or twice. He appeared to be having quite a session with someone. He came back in the end and sat in the passenger seat with me. His big face told me nothing in the light from the dashboard. I offered him a cigarette. He declined it politely. I lit one myself anyway.

'Sounds like a malicious,' he said eventually. 'We get dozens. Some party phoned in a while back, reporting a suspicious car with your number. Something about a body. Even told us where you'd be on the highway.'

'Seems they missed out,' I said mechanically. 'Sorry I can't oblige.'

The big cop's face split open in a grin. 'We can't always be lucky,' he said.

He got out and went round to my driving door.

'If you get a line on the joker,' I said, 'I'd like to know who he is.'

He scratched his shoulder where the heavy

straps of his uniform crossed it. He spat disgustedly.

'Hardly likely, Mr Faraday. Anonymous tip-off from a phone-booth, like always. Man's voice. Nothing to go on. Like always again. But we got to follow them all up.'

'Sure,' I said. 'Anyway, if you do hear, you know where to reach me.'

He nodded. 'Thanks for your co-operation. Some citizens get mighty het up over these little checks.'

I smiled. 'Nothing you can't handle,' I said, looking at his six feet six of solid bone and muscle.

O'Rourke smiled too. 'Nothing I can't handle,' he said. 'Be seeing you.'

He went back to his machine, took it down off the stand and kicked it into thunderous life. He pulled slowly out into the traffic stream, waved once and was then lost in the myriad lights rolling into L.A. I sat on and smoked for a few minutes, thinking over the evening.

Then I drove into L.A. at a more leisurely pace.

Chapter Seven

Bishop's Palace

1

When I got to the office next morning I found a pencilled note from Stella: Had to go out for half an hour. Cardinal Bishop rang.

She gave the number to call. I looked at my watch. It was around 9.30 a.m. and the sun spilling in through the blinds was already beginning to heat the room up. It didn't look like too good a start to the day.

I opened a window, took off my jacket, sat down at my desk and went through the few letters and bills Stella had left on my blotter. Then I rang Bishop's number. He didn't sound any prettier than he looked.

'You took your time,' he grumbled.

'It's my time,' I agreed with him, 'so don't waste it.'

'Some partner,' he said mournfully.

'That's your idea, not mine,' I said.

He ignored that. I looked down at the blotter and saw that Stella had left me a cardboard folder, one of the numbered ones we used for filing information. I opened it, listening to Bishop's heavy breathing at the other end of the line. There was a letter from

Davidson in it and the stuff I'd asked for; there were photostats of Kovacs' truck record sheets, a photostat of his company file, even a list of Davidson's truck drivers.

'You there, Faraday?' said Bishop petulantly in my ear.

'I never go to sleep on the job,' I said.

He snorted. 'I thought it was about time we got together,' he said. 'Pool our ideas.'

'Since when did you have any ideas?' I said.

'Aw, don't be like that, Mr Faraday,' he whined. 'There might be a lot in this for both of us if we handle it right.'

'Good of you to use the plural,' I said.

He went on like he hadn't heard my end of the dialogue.

'I haven't been idle,' he said. 'I thought you'd like to come over. We could split a bottle.'

'This time of the morning?' I asked. I could imagine Bishop's brand of horse liniment.

'It was just an idea,' he whined.

'Keep it like that,' I advised him. 'I could look over later but it had better be worth the journey.'

'Fine,' he said. 'I got an office on Cahengua Boulevard. Number 246. First floor back.'

'Sounds swell,' I said insincerely.

'You didn't tell the police anything?' he asked.

'About what?' I said.

He breathed heavily again for a moment

or two.

'I can see how you got your reputation,' he said. 'Real discreet.'

'Save the flattery,' I told him. 'Just stick to the paper work and let me do the real stuff.'

I put down the phone before he started bleating again. I studied the papers Stella had left for me. It was a little cooler in the office now. Either the open window had done the trick or the janitor had got the air conditioning working again.

The note from Davidson detailed the sites Kovacs was working on when he disappeared and the routes he would normally have taken. Davidson had even given the names of Kovacs' two closest partners among the other truck drivers, together with their private addresses. These were two men called Kelly and Remick; I noted their trucks had been working on the same job as Kovacs.

I'd had Stella run a check on missing persons but no-one answering Kovacs' description had been found dead or reported to the L.A. Police recently. Apparently Kovacs had no family to worry about him; he was a single man and lived in the same rooming house as Remick and Kelly.

I left word for Stella where I could be found and drove across town to Bishop's place. On the way over I stopped and bought an Examiner. I went in a coffee shop and sat with the paper for a quarter of an hour. I went through it carefully but I couldn't find even an inch of type on the bald-headed man being found where I'd dumped him. I felt the situation would be under control for a week or so. And by then anything could have happened. Like me disappearing myself. I remembered again the marksman up the canyon. I paid the check and went out. Twice I caught myself looking in the driving mirror on the way across town.

2

Cahengua Boulevard wasn't any great shakes as a business section. It wasn't slum but neither was it Grade A real estate. It was just plain seedy. I drove along until I found a slot in the traffic and sneaked in on a lot behind a board-walk, risking my fenders between a parked truck and a 1938 Dodge some joker had painted in zebra stripes of blue, white and yellow. I killed the motor and walked back a couple of blocks. Number 246 was a shabby glassed-in entrance porch between a drug-store and a leather goods shop.

I walked in across a cheap oil-cloth floored hall to the big, dusty staircase with its old-fashioned balustrade. There was no elevator so I walked up. It was so dark on the first floor that they kept the electric light on all day. Naked bulbs of low wattage burned in cheap plastic shades on the fusty landing. Business

61

cards were pinned to a baize-covered board at one side of the corridor. I walked over and studied it. I figured that people who consulted Bishop would need twenty-twenty vision if they wanted to make out.

I found his card, a large piece of cheap pasteboard, curled at the edges and yellowed with age. It said: CARDINAL BISHOP. Confidential Investigations Undertaken. Divorce and Private Enquiries a Speciality. I grinned at the card and went on down the hall. Room 11 was like Bishop had said, on the first floor back. The atmosphere in here was stale and heavy with the odours of dust, cheap perfume and canned beer. Through the clear tops of windows whose lower halves were heavily frosted I could see the blank yellow bricks of a tenement opposite. None of the windows were open, despite the heat of the day.

A dirty piece of paper pinned to the door I wanted said: Cardinal Bishop. Knock and Enter.

I knocked and went on in. It wasn't the F.B.I., but then I wasn't expecting anything much. So I wasn't disappointed. Four off-yellow walls, a faded carpet, a broken-down black leather settee whose springs were showing, a dusty framed diploma on the wall. Bishop sat at a desk that looked like a converted kitchen table and tried to seem important. Several wire trays were stacked up with material that looked like preliminary reports on the assassination of Abraham Lincoln.

There were two grimy windows set in back of the office, that looked on to the same yellow brick tenements; the bottoms of the windows were frosted and black letters stencilled on to the windows in reverse repeated the legend on the board in the hall. I wondered who would be able to read them at that height. Pigeons, perhaps. Two green metal filing cabinets, a telephone, a couple of ladder-back chairs completed the furnishings. I almost felt sorry for Bishop. The feeling didn't last long.

I walked over towards Bishop's desk carefully; I was afraid I might go through the floor and it was quite a way down. Dust rose from the carpet under my feet. There was another hard chair set in front of Bishop's desk. I could see that had woodworm in it so I didn't sit down in too much of a hurry. Bishop fumbled with his papers a moment longer; this was the busy routine that made out his time was worth a dollar a minute. I figured he thought I was a client.

'Don't waste the material,' I said. 'I'm not a paying customer.'

Bishop jumped like he'd been stung. Then he contorted his face up into one of his famous smiles.

'Great!' he said. 'I'm glad you could make it.'

He opened a drawer in his desk and fished around; I could hear the clink of glass on glass. He came up with a bottle with a yellow label and two badly smeared tumblers. Bishop uncorked the bottle and poured some of the fluid into the tumblers. He pushed one across the desk to me. I sniffed it.

'What's this? Paint stripper?' I said.

Bishop sighed. He got another bottle out of the desk.

'I got something better here,' he said. He took back the tumbler and tipped it into his own glass. He uncorked the new bottle and slopped some of its contents into my tumbler. This one had a mauve label. I studied it.

'Algerian reisling,' I said. 'No thanks.'

Bishop scowled. 'You don't go by the label,' he said. 'I got this special out of bond. There isn't much of this about.'

I refrained from making the obvious remark.

'Suit yourself,' Bishop said. He drank. It didn't seem to do him any actual harm. His gold teeth winked in the light of the overhead bulb as he tipped the glass. He smacked his lips and poured himself another slug. He must have had a stomach like an ostrich. He scratched his sandy hair reflectively; he looked like a pineapple sitting smugly behind the desk.

He shot me a shifty glance. 'No Kovacs?' he said nervously.

64

'No Kovacs,' I said.

'But you've got something to work on?' Bishop continued.

'I've got plenty to work on,' I said, remembering the man with jug ears, a bullet sparking off rock, Professor Hilton, April Dawn and a customs post smack in the middle of American territory. Not to mention helicopters and anonymous phone-calls. I sighed heavily. I had no shortage of loose ends on this case. Bishop sucked his teeth noisily as he drained his tumbler. He set it down on the table in front of him, squinted at it like it had the answer to his problems.

'Now let's see what you came up with,' I said.

Bishop shifted in the chair.

'You haven't told me nuthin' yet,' he complained.

'It's the way I work,' I said.

He looked at me greedily. 'Davidson didn't come up with anything?' he asked eagerly.

I stared at him for a long moment. 'He just paid you, remember? So why would he want to pay twice—for no results and no information.'

Bishop lowered his face to the desk again, uncorked the bottle and poured himself another rat-poison.

'Sure, sure,' he mumbled. 'I just wondered. I forgot.'

'You don't forget when it comes to your split,' I told him.

Bishop stared at me from under half-open lids. 'You want a cut on account?' he asked.

'On account of what,' I said. 'Save your money. You're going to need it for all those cab-fares.'

'What cab-fares?' he asked suspiciously.

'For all that hard work you're going to do on this case,' I said.

Bishop scowled. It made his previous expressions seem like sunshine on a clear July day. He fished in a drawer of his desk and came up with a grubby brown envelope. He grunted like the exertion had exhausted him. He slammed the drawer shut with his gut and flipped the envelope over towards me.

'I already been making with the hard work,' he said aggressively.

'Oh,' I said politely. I opened the envelope. It contained a typewritten report. I had to admit it did look like Bishop had been doing something to earn his money. Apart from the grammatical faults and the illiterate spelling, it wasn't bad value so far as Davidson was concerned. Except that it didn't get the case much farther forward. My expression must have given me away for Bishop said hastily, 'That's just the rough. I got an agency that puts the education in the finished report.'

I went down it rapidly; Bishop had apparently interviewed three of the truck drivers who had known Kovacs best. I came across the names of Kelly and Remick again; it was beginning to sound like a music hall act. There wasn't much in the report I didn't already know; thin stuff to justify my coming over. I figured Bishop was more interested in what I might have to tell him. I put the report in the envelope and pushed it back towards him. I got out a package and lit a cigarette; I offered one to Bishop but he waved it away.

His little eyes studied me anxiously; the gold teeth glinted again as he licked his lips.

'You got a lead on this character who tried to jump you?' he asked. I shook my head. I thought it over and then decided not to tell him about the kill. He might pass out and I didn't want that on my conscience. I didn't tell him about April Dawn and her uncle either. Instead I described jug-ears and waited for Bishop's reaction. I was disappointed. The information obviously didn't mean a thing to him.

Bishop licked his lips again. 'You think this bimbo got rid of Kovacs' body?'

'It's possible,' I admitted. 'You remember passing a house up there with a Chinese gateway?'

I drew the shape of the gateway in the air with my hands. Bishop thought for a moment. Then his face cleared.

'Yeah, I remember,' he said. 'The place with green shutters. Why? Something wrong with it?'

I decided to level with Bishop for a minute

or two, just to see if he had anything to give.

'It might have been used by the character who jumped me as a sort of observation post,' I said.

Bishop nodded like he had it all figured out a long time ago. It meant nothing. I'd seen Oliver Hardy do the same thing in too many movies to be fooled. Bishop hadn't an idea what I was talking about.

'Maybe the truck drivers were tipping stuff where they shouldn't,' I went on patiently. 'Somewhere people didn't want strangers snooping.'

Bishop's face cleared. 'You might of got something there, Mr Faraday,' he said, with what passed for eagerness in him. 'You want for me to stake the place out?'

I put down my cigarette on the lid of an old typewriter ribbon tin that served him for an ashtray and fought down the temptation to strangle him where he sat.

'That's exactly what I don't want you to do,' I said at length.

'You've been up there once already, remember? And you know what happened then.'

Bishop gulped and the colour came and went on his fat cheeks. 'I'm not likely to forget,' he said.

'That's all right, then,' I said. 'Leave the Warner Brothers stuff to me.'

Bishop drained some more of the nauseous

liquid in his glass and wrinkled up his nose in appreciation.

'What do you want me to do, Mr Faraday?' he asked.

'I've put down a few routine things for you,' I said. I passed over to him a typewritten list of items I'd had Stella prepare; stuff that would keep him out of mischief but at the same time let him think he was earning his fee.

To my surprise he broke into a broad smile.

'Sure, Mr Faraday,' he said, going down the list rapidly, with a shrewd eye. 'Anything you say. You want me to contact you if anything breaks?'

'Only if it's important,' I said. 'Otherwise I'll be in touch.'

I got up and went to the door; he didn't say anything else. I looked back before I went out. He had uncorked the bottle again and was re-filling his glass. The air was close and stuffy and a single beam of sunlight was struggling to overcome the trail of dust my footsteps had evoked from the carpet. In a way it had been a wasted morning but I'd learned one thing; unless Bishop was the finest actor in the world.

There was a gurgling noise as Bishop put the tumbler to his mouth. I closed the door softly behind me and beat it down the stairs towards the fresh air.

Chapter Eight

City Dump

1

The motor under the bright yellow bonnet of the big truck throbbed heavily; the warmth of the engine came up and mingled with the heat of the day so that the farther sheds and bays of Davidson's yard rippled and shifted like a mirage. Lee Kelly came round the bonnet wiping his hands on a piece of coarse waste. The oil left thick dark streaks on the grey of the cotton.

'So what's your theory, Mr Faraday?' he said.

'I haven't got one,' I said. 'I've never met Kovacs. He was your friend, wasn't he?'

Kelly finishing wiping his hands and put the waste in a pocket of his blue coveralls; he was a big, broad-shouldered man in his mid-forties with black hair that was now receding at the temples. He had a tough, good-humoured face and strong, square teeth showed when he opened his mouth to smile, which was often.

'Not a friend,' he said cautiously. 'He rooms in the same place and we work for the same outfit, of course. But he was a pretty close guy; he didn't confide in any of us.'

'Known him long?' I asked.

Kelly lifted the bonnet, using the cotton waste to touch the metal; he fiddled with the oil dipstick, a worried look on his face. He wiped the dipstick on the waste and then put it back into the sump.

'I been with Alcazar three years,' he said, 'and Kovacs was here before me. He's a good truckie, but too fast for my money. I figured he'd sail on over the top of a ravine one of these days.'

I finished buttoning up the top of my own coverall, which Davidson had issued me with. 'Meaning what?'

Kelly took the dipstick out of the engine and studied the oil level on it; his face cleared and he put it back and closed the bonnet with a clang.

'Kovacs was keen on money,' he said. 'He had a wife somewhere in the East and a fancy piece here in L.A.'

He wiped his hands on the cotton waste and gazed out across the yard where the heat-haze shimmered on the runs of baking hot concrete.

'So?' I prompted him.

Kelly turned to face me; he took a long blue baseball cap out of his rear pocket, unfolded it and put it on his head; the protruding peak and the shadow it cast on his face gave him a strangely cadaverous look. He took a pair of dark goggles from off the seat of the open driving cab before he replied.

'So Kovacs took chances,' he answered at length. 'His runs were always a third under time of the average driver here. So he did more hauls per day and he always volunteered for extra runs or overtime if there was any going.'

'So he might have been engaged in illegal dumping on this project?' I said.

Kelly climbed up into the big cab and stood looking down at me; he had to raise his voice above the throb of the motor.

'I didn't say that,' he said defensively.

I went round to the passenger side of the cab and got up, using the step and the handrail. It seemed a long way; when I was in the cab next to Kelly the view from the driver's window made us seem almost invincible. My Buick, parked the other side of the yard, looked like a plastic toy.

'No, but you implied it,' I said. 'My name's not Davidson. I'm not interested in your working practices. I'm merely digging for myself.'

Kelly leaned forward and checked the instrument panel in front of him. He nodded.

The heat was stifling in the cab; Kelly pushed a switch and set a fan going. It merely re-distributed the heated air. I opened the window on my side as wide as it would go.

'I don't know what Kovacs did,' Kelly said. 'He didn't let on to us. But some of us suspected he might have been dumping in illegal locations to save time. There's lots of places up and down the canyons. But you can't do it too often because the owners of the ground often call the police in or stake out the place themselves. It's not worth losing the job and you get a bad reputation among the truck operators.'

'Where do you think Kovacs might have been dumping?' I asked. Kelly shrugged his broad shoulders.

'I'll leave you to figure that out, Mr Faraday. You're the detective. I just do the driving. Do you want a special run or just the regular?'

'Do like always,' I said. 'Just pretend I'm not here.'

Kelly grinned. 'Okay, Mr Faraday. Hold on to your hat.'

I was already sweating inside the coveralls. 'You should've taken off your tie and rolled up your shirt-sleeves,' he said. 'These boxes get pretty hot this time of year.'

'I'm strictly a white-collar boy,' I said.

Kelly grinned again. 'Those coveralls won't fool anybody on this trip, Mr Faraday,' he said.

'Never mind,' I told him. 'Maybe they'll figure I'm the boss's son learning the business the hard way.'

Kelly spat easily out the window; he waved up towards Davidson's office building as we rolled through the gate. The vibration and noise in here was terrific. I wedged myself against the padded bench and braced my legs

73

up on the sloping front of the cab.

'You'll get used to it,' Kelly said. 'You get used to anything. Take me for instance. I been at this game nearly thirty years.'

'I don't aim to make a career of it,' I said. 'Wonder you weren't shaken to pieces years ago.'

Kelly spun the wheel expertly to miss a bump in the rough road. 'Who says I ain't?' he asked no-one in particular.

I got out a route-map and studied it. Davidson had seconded Kelly to me for the day; I hadn't told him why I was along, except to ask him a few questions. I really wanted to find out how much ground Kovacs could have saved by dumping in Tintoretto Canyon. It was my guess no-one knew about the canyon kill except me and Bishop and the guy who hit Kovacs—if he was dead. But remembering jug-ears I didn't give much for his chances.

I was beginning to believe Bishop in some instances; but looked at any way this case was as lousy as they come. The only body we had was the wrong one; and I couldn't spill that without incriminating myself. For the moment I just had to soldier on with Bishop as a doubtful partner and hope for a lucky break. And lucky breaks weren't exactly plentiful on the ground this season.

Kelly pulled the big truck out of the side road from Davidson's place on to the main highway; he handled it like he was born to the

74

business. While I was fighting every jolt and crash he was riding easily, seemingly glued to his seat, making the whole thing look simple; I consoled myself by thinking he would have a hell of an uncomfortable ride in a Rolls.

He pulled expertly round an elderly matron in a red rose-petal hat who was dawdling behind the wheel of an opulent green Packard sedan. She looked surprised as her windscreen disappeared in the dust; Kelly grinned into the rear mirror as he saw the Packard start to wobble and lose way. He said something unprintable into the hot wind that came in his side of the cab; I gathered it was about women drivers.

We drove ten miles across the sad city, jammed in at intersections with automobiles that looked like so many sardine-cans in their similarity; the throbbing of their exhausts and the thin blue smoke that choked the lungs and made the eyes smart, even at the height of the cab, made the journey a delight. I usually avoided that route this time of day; Kelly smiled sardonically to himself. He'd put on dark glasses that fitted closely to his cheekbones; with the exhaust fumes and the smog he'd need them on this run.

He turned off at the next crossing and cut down a quiet residential section; he drove fast, but well, just within the legal limits, but I noticed he didn't lose any time at all in getting from A to B. It was nearly an hour before we got to the Algonquin housing project; about thirty acres hacked out of the solid hillside. Bulldozers were turning up the dusty earth and a scarlet crane pecked about in the desolate, man-made landscape. Kelly pulled up a dirt road and got in a queue behind four other giant dump trucks; at the head of the line a scoop on a front-end loader savaged great chunks of earth and rock from where it had been piled and dropped it thunderously into the first truck, slice by slice.

Kelly switched off his motor and we sat smoking until it was time to pull up again; the first dump truck went lumbering away, the second started to fill and the process was repeated. I figured the halt cost us thirty minutes before it was our turn to load. The cab shook as hundredweights of rubble and shale cascaded into the steel-lined box behind our cab. The negro operating the front-end loader gave us a brilliant smile; he was naked except for his jeans and rope-soled sandals and the sweat cascaded down his ebony body, reflecting back points of white light from the blinding glare of the sun.

Kelly finished off his cigarette as the racket went on and the cab swayed around us; he stubbed out the butt in the metal ashtray on the dash. I saw it was three-quarters full already. I could feel the sweat working its way down my own body under the thick coveralls. White dust swirled in at the window, raked by the burning wind from off the hillside.

'Some living, eh?' said Kelly grimly, more to himself than to me. The negro dumped the last slice in the back of our truck and left his machine running. He went over to a stand pipe and sluiced himself down from a green plastic hosepipe; the water looked cool and good against the skin of his powerful shoulders. He grinned again and waved. Kelly forked his fingers at him good-naturedly; the negro's smile widened until it seemed to bisect the whole width of his face. His body was almost dry before he'd got back up on his seat again.

The next truck moved up behind us as Kelly gunned the motor, letting in the clutch slowly to take up the enormous load; the cab shuddered as Kelly spun the wheel, easing the tons of earth and rock judderingly over the rough track to turn around and head back the way we'd come. I braced my feet against the front of the cab and wondered why I was along this afternoon. I knew why but I could have got the same information with a quarter of the discomfort; except that this was part of my make-up. Doing things the hard way. I sighed and concentrated on keeping upright as the cab started to gyrate in what seemed an uncontrollable manner as Kelly picked up speed as we got down off the hillside.

He turned through the residential section and then picked another route; I followed it on my map as he twisted and turned across the baking city. I put my window up as the smog and the exhaust fumes increased; Kelly made good time nevertheless and I noticed that every obscure side-road that would give him a minute or two of time was utilised; I guessed he had done this run a hundred times. The trip had been something like two and a quarter hours including time to site and for waiting and loading, before we reached the dumping place. Kelly spun the wheel again and we were running in between the high, mouldering walls of warehouses; from far off the high, thin siren of a freight train blew. We jolted across rails that shone like molten metal in the bright light of the afternoon sun and were then going downhill.

We were near the shore, in an area of flat land where much of the city's garbage was dumped; the big truck rumbled along a cinder track that wound between towering heaps of malodorous refuse. Paper flapped mournfully in the breeze and the salt smell of the sea brought with it other odours not so pleasant; thin flame burnt on the tips, mingled with smoke like white steam from spontaneous combustion. A few human figures poked aimlessly at the mounds of rubble like the survivors of Hiroshima.

Two more Alcazar trucks were ahead of us at the dumping point, close to the shore, where the garbage was being covered over with earth and debris, so we had to queue again. Kelly switched off the motor and we smoked.

'You need a lot of patience in this business,' I said.

Kelly smiled. He looked out to where gulls swooped and screamed over scraps of food near the edge of the sea.

'It can be a hard life, being a truckie,' he said, 'but it's free and the money's good. I get by making three trips a day like this.' He tapped the butt of his cigarette on the dashboard, to make the tobacco even. He wet the paper with the edge of his tongue. 'You know how many Kovacs does in a day?'

I didn't answer but sat with my side window open, making good use of the slight breeze from the direction of the sea.

'Six, maybe seven,' Kelly answered for me. He stared moodily out of the window to where the second Alcazar truck backed up to the tipping edge; the other bounced back up along the trackway we'd come in.

'You saw how long it's taken us today,' said Kelly, 'and we didn't waste any time. You can't do that many trips playing by the rules.'

He drew on his cigarette and put it down on the edge of the ashtray in the dash; he had a gimmick there made of two bent paper clips that held the butt of the cigarette and prevented it from falling. He switched on the engine; the cab juddered again as he backed the truck up to the position just vacated by the one in front. The other driver waved as he went round in back of us. Kelly judged his distance and reversed out until it seemed to me that the rear of the truck was dangerously over-hanging the steep slope of the tip; it went down to the water's edge in a sort of lagoon in which the decayed heaps of city refuse and the tipped rubble were like islands.

Kelly left the engine running and put on the brakes. He moved two levers set into a gear box midway between him and me; the cab vibrated as the hydraulic jacks started shoving the tons of load upwards. I looked out the rear window of the cab which was just being obscured as the truck body was raised almost vertical. The racket was deafening as the earth and rubble slid over the steel-shod floor of the truck and down the hillside. Kelly grunted as the last of the load disappeared. He reversed the tipping mechanism and waited until the truck body was horizontal; three more trucks had come up by this time.

Then he put the gear in and we rolled slowly up the hill away towards the grimy sky and the jagged outlines of the fringe of the city. I sat and sweated and finished my cigarette and went on marking my map. Back in the suburbs Kelly parked the truck on a lot already half-filled with heavy transport; we went in a truckies' cafe that was a mixture of big, sweaty men, blue smoke and schooners of beer. We found seats in a booth and got the ice-cold lager down us.

Kelly wiped the froth from his lips with a meaty red hand and reached for another cigarette; I passed him one of mine.

'Well, I hope you got what you came for, Mr Faraday,' he said morosely.

'I got what I came for,' I said.

Presently we climbed back in the cab and Kelly drove on over to Alcazar; it was out of his way but he insisted. He dropped me at the gate and left for another run up to the housing site. I thanked him and went across the yard and into a square, white-tiled truckies' washroom that was empty this time of the afternoon. I hung up the coveralls in a steel blue-painted locker that Davidson had allocated me and ran a cold tap on my face. After I'd washed up I changed into my own clothes and left the locker open with the key in the door; I went on out, got the Buick and drove back to my office. I'd learned one thing, at any rate. The route Kelly had taken between the housing site and the dumping area had passed a mile to the east of Tintoretto Canyon which explained why Kovacs had been able to make so many journeys. It cut nearly 10 miles off the trip.

2

Stella sat opposite me and tapped with a pencil against very white teeth. Her eyes searched my face like they could read everything going on inside my skull; very likely they could. But it wouldn't have done Stella much good. There was very little going on inside my skull right now. Leastways, anything that would be any help on this case. So far it rated Grade Z in my record book. I frowned across at the large-scale map of L.A. that concealed our flimsy wall safe; the answer was somewhere there up Tintoretto Canyon. And something told me this was an assignment I wouldn't get rich on. Not the way Cardinal Bishop was shaping up.

Stella rose suddenly; she went over to the alcove and started rattling around with cups and saucers.

'I thought it was about time,' I said.

'You thought nothing,' said Stella. 'You were miles away. If I didn't feed you coffee and biscuits occasionally you'd starve yourself to death.'

I grinned. I went on smoking and studying Stella's legs in the telephone mirror. They were the best legs in the world and Stella was as nice as they come; they don't come any nicer but somehow I never could get around to saying yes to her. Which made the office an area where an interesting explosion could take place any time. Stella turned round while I was thinking this and I snapped the mirror shut and slid it back into the little tray at the bottom of the instrument.

'And don't think you're fooling me any, chum,' she said.

'I ate just this afternoon,' I said defensively.

'I didn't mean that,' said Stella patiently. 'I'm talking about something else. This girl April Shower.'

'Dawn,' I corrected her.

'Anyway, whatever her name is,' Stella said darkly, 'I don't think I like her.'

'You've never met her,' I said.

'You never bring that kind to the office,' she said. She went back to the alcove and started pouring boiling water on to the coffee grounds; the aroma went clear through the open window and down on to the boulevard.

'Afraid of competition?' I asked.

Stella arched her back; she turned her profile to me as she stirred the coffee decisively. Her breasts strained against the blue and white striped blouse she wore; I figured they would just fit nicely in the palms of my two hands one day. Stella ran a soft hand over an immaculate knee with an electric shirring of caressed stocking that sent up my pulse-rate. She stood for a moment, her honey-blonde hair shimmering in the sunlight that spilled in through the open window.

'What do you think, Mike?' she asked, her pink tongue exploring her full lips.

'For Christ's sake,' I said irritably. 'You know what I think. Come and sit down and stop preening yourself. It's too hot for that stuff.'

Stella smiled in a self-satisfied manner.

'Well, well,' she said to herself. 'The man is human after all.'

She came over and set the coffee down on the blotter at my elbow. She went behind me and fooled gently with my ear. I could stand just so much of that. I reached in back for her but she skipped out too quickly. Stella had gotten used to my reflexes and my breaking-point pretty accurately by now. She went and got her own coffee and sat down at the desk opposite me. She rested her head on her two hands and looked at me quizzically.

'You're holding something back.'

'You could say that,' I said. I stirred my coffee and inhaled the fresh aroma. Coffee was something I never got tired of; Stella and I drank it in the office to the exclusion of everything else, even all through the long, hot summers. It was to us what nectar used to be to the ancient gods. Except that the ancient gods hadn't got Stella to do the brewing up. And that was a definite disadvantage.

Stella got out her scratch pad as I started talking. She sipped at the coffee, took notes and gazed at me disapprovingly from time to time as I went on. I didn't miss anything out. She made a moue when I got to the part about my uninvited car passenger. I expected an outburst but just then the phone buzzed and saved me. Stella reached for the phone, listened for a moment and cupped her hand over the mouthpiece.

'Spring's a little early this year,' she said.

I picked up my phone. 'This is April,' the girl's voice said. She sounded remote, strained. 'Can we talk openly?'

'What can I do for you?' I asked. 'There's only my secretary here and she's practically my mother-confessor.'

Stella smiled sardonically. She put down her own phone with a rattle. Her high heels tip-tapped aggressively across the office as she went to the alcove to wash the cups and saucers.

'I must see you, Mike,' the girl went on. 'Something's come up. I can't talk now. I'm in town. About nine o'clock this evening?'

She gave her address as the Park-Plaza Apartments. I took down the room number.

'I'll be there,' I promised. I put back the phone and lit a cigarette. Stella came back and picked up my coffee cup and took it away. Her manner was deceptively calm but there were bright lights dancing in her eyes. I copied out the Park-Plaza details and put them down next to her scratch pad so that she could put the information on file.

'All right,' I said. 'I should have reported the death to the police. It's all too complicated to go into now. And even with McGiver or Captain Dan Tucker down at County Police H.Q. it's going to be difficult to explain away.'

Stella smiled. 'I know,' she said. 'You'll get to it later. Like always.'

'Well,' I said defensively, 'when I've found what's going on up Tintoretto Canyon and why you need passports to get from one part of California to another, that'll be time to get the law in.'

'Sure,' said Stella but her tone of voice wasn't convincing. 'Look after yourself, Mike.'

She came up close to me and kissed me on the side of the face. I didn't encourage her. But at the same time I wasn't exactly resisting. I fought against it for about five seconds. When we came out of the clinch I said, 'I don't think there's any physical danger about going up to the Park-Plaza.'

'I didn't mean that,' said Stella in a tone of voice I'd heard before. 'I was talking about April Dawn.'

'What do you take me for?' I asked, using a pocket handkerchief on my face.

'I won't answer that,' said Stella.

She was still standing smiling as I went out the door.

Chapter Nine

Love and Hisses

1

It was a quarter of nine when I stopped the Buick in a cement parking lot bordered by carefully shaved lawns and azalea beds. The Park-Plaza Apartments was a two-block, black glass and white concrete box set down in four acres of ornamental gardens. Copper-fluted fountains played in marble basins in the front concourse. I went up the broad entrance steps feeling like I ought to have worn my best pair of corsets. There was lilac flooring in the entrance hall and another fountain here too.

A woman in black silk with a white lace collar sat behind a sapele kiosk bordered with plastic flowers, wearing an expression like a constipated nun. I could smell her disapproval all the way from here to Kansas City and back as I gave her the number of April Dawn's suite. She pressed a button on the desk in front of her and reached for a gold Swedish telephone that looked like something out of the Year 3000.

'She's expecting me,' I said brightly.

The black silk job looked me up and down. Her face was like a kettle on the boil.

'No doubt,' she said tartly. 'There's a Mr Faraday here to see you, Miss Dawn,' she said venomously into the mouthpiece. She put the instrument down with an incredulous expression.

'She said you're to go right up,' she murmured in a dazed voice.

'Looks like it's my evening,' I told her. I cracked her a wide smile and went on across the lobby to where half a dozen elevator cages were waiting for customers. I got into the nearest and thumbed the button. I whined upwards to the tenth floor and got out. Two-four-zero was down a long corridor and up green marble steps. The suite was the last door and a big floor to ceiling window at the end of the passage made a frame for the garish lights of L.A. spread out below; like always the smog made the picture blurred but this was one of the better nights. The traffic made long white, yellow and scarlet worms of light which threaded their way through the miles of neon. It wasn't the most beautiful view in the world but it meant home to me.

I was standing thinking about nothing and taking in the lights and the automobiles and the night and the smog when I heard the door click; the apartment was visible through the open door. April Dawn was standing in the entrance. She had on a white silk house coat with a red Chinese pattern on it. She looked back along the corridor; her face was pale in the shaded lamps. She took me by the arm.

'Come on in, Mike. You weren't followed?'

Her voice trembled. She seemed close to tears.

'Not so far as I know,' I said. 'Why, should I be?'

She closed the door behind us, turned the key in the lock and put the chain on the bronze metal slide which retained it.

'I'm worried,' she said. The room we were in was a big one and had a fine view of all the smog from the picture window. There was a narrow balcony out front with wrought iron furniture and beach umbrellas anchored to the terrace in metal holders. There was only one shaded lamp burning in the corner of the room. April Dawn went over and drew the curtains.

'I'm sorry,' she said. 'I was forgetting myself. You'd like a drink?'

'Sure,' I said. 'If it's convenient.'

She switched on another lamp. By the stronger light I could see she really looked worried.

'Why wouldn't it be?' she said.

I sat down in a black leather armchair and looked around the apartment. It was done out as a living room with expensive hand-made wallpaper blocked out to look like grass and small china ornaments and other water fowl on glass shelving around the walls. Together with April Dawn's dressing gown it increased the

Oriental effect.

'I don't know,' I said. 'There's something funny about this set-up.'

April Dawn pushed back her blonde hair from in front of her eyes with an impatient gesture.

'I'm all upset tonight, Mike,' she said. 'If you'll give me a few minutes.'

'Sure,' I said. 'Just take your time. I'll have that drink now if you don't mind.'

She got a decanter off the table and poured the bourbon; she put ice in with an unsteady hand. The tongs clattered on the side of the glass. I got up and prowled around the room while she was doing this. I pretended to examine the water fowl but I was looking for other exits in the apartment. There was another door at the far end which might have been a bathroom; a door facing me across the width of the room was ajar and the room beyond was obviously a bedroom.

There was still something not quite right; I looked through into the bedroom as I passed. There was a big bed with a blue silk coverlet and a large table lamp burning at the side of the bed; the lamp was in the shape of a blue china vase to match the bed cover and had a white silk shade. The drapes at the window, which looked on to the terrace, were drawn. I went back to the living room and took the drink April Dawn handed me.

'Here's how,' she said. I went and sat down

again on the black leather armchair and waited for her to begin. She licked her lips nervously and sat down on a plush stool opposite my chair; she put her drink on a small round mahogany table at her elbow.

'Where was I, Mike?' she said.

'You were in some trouble,' I told her. I sipped the bourbon and studied her over the rim of my glass.

'God knows it's true, Mike,' she said. 'I'm in deep and I don't know how to get out.'

'That's what I'm in business for,' I said. 'To listen to other people's problems.'

'It's not only that,' she said. 'You're in deep too. I'm part of it. But I happen to like you. And that I didn't bargain for.'

She looked at me with dark eyes full of pain. Her lips trembled momentarily and then she had control of herself. She picked up her glass again and drank to steady her nerves.

'We aren't what we seem,' she said enigmatically.

'I know,' I told her. 'The house at Tintoretto Canyon is a blind for something else. A sort of gateway to keep people out.'

Her eyes opened and her mouth made a silent 0 in the whiteness of her face.

'I told Trygon it was madness,' she said. 'That it would never work. But he's insane. And he has absolute power. The truck drivers were only the beginning.'

'Don't you think that's where you'd better

91

start, April?' I said. 'Right at the beginning.'

She nodded. She stood up suddenly. 'Let's go inside,' she said. 'I've got some papers I want you to see.'

She indicated the open door behind her. I picked up my glass and followed her in. A faint breeze rustled the curtains in the semi-tropical night; the scent of jasmine came from somewhere, deadening the gasoline fumes. I stood in the open doorway and watched while she went over to a bureau and fiddled with a key in the lock.

'Just where does Professor Hilton figure in all this?' I asked.

'He's no relative, if that's what you mean,' she said in a dead voice.

'I'd already worked that one out for myself,' I said.

She didn't seem at all surprised. She turned the key in the bureau lock. 'Trygon gets the best. He knows how to pay. And when he's finished with people then they go straight out without trace.'

'Like Kovacs,' I said. 'Sounds like a nice fellow.'

April Dawn opened the bureau drawer, took some papers out and turned towards me.

'Kovacs?' she said, wrinkling up her forehead.

'The truck driver,' I said. 'The one who got killed up at Tintoretto just a short while ago. The reason I got drawn into this. Mr Trygon's doing, no doubt.'

April Dawn cleared her throat and sat down awkwardly on the bed with the blue coverlet; she crossed her legs and turned towards me, pushing back her blonde hair from her eyes.

'What's your theory, Mike?'

'I'm a simple guy,' I said. 'Let's say there's something peculiar up the canyon. Something that calls for customs posts and passport controls. Plus some sort of private army in uniforms and with tommy guns. You and Hilton in the house to keep an eye on things. Mr Trygon, whoever he is, pulling the strings. Until truck drivers start tearing fences down, dumping their loads on Trygon's land in order to shortcut on contracts and earn bigger bonuses. But Trygon can't afford that. It might uncover his racket. So his boys kill the truckie Kovacs, steal his truck and hide the body. But not before somebody has spotted it. Someone who came along while the tough characters were away. Leaving a sentry who couldn't do anything about it. Like a girl, perhaps.'

April Dawn started and a pink patch came and went on each cheek. She took a cigarette box off a table near the bed. The thin scrape of the match against the edge of the box as she lit the cigarette seemed to scrape at my nerves as well.

'Go on,' she said softly.

'In the meantime the boys have dumped the truck and the body. In a swamp perhaps, on

93

Trygon's land. And he's got miles of land to play with. But someone knows. Question is, who.'

I took a cigarette from the box April Dawn handed me and put it to my lips. I leaned forward as she pressed the glowing end of her own cigarette against mine. I puffed in silence for a minute or two; neons made a green and gold dazzle through a gap in the bedroom curtains to the side of us.

'The guy who spotted the body doesn't keep it to himself. He comes to me. And when I turn up you're ready. One of Trygon's best men is on the job. But he goofs. I get away and Trygon puts the chill on him. It was quite a good idea planting the body in my car and tipping off the police. It got rid of two nuisances in one. As it happened I only just made it.'

The girl smiled. 'I thought you were pretty good, Mike, when I first met you. What did you do with the body?'

I puffed out smoke. 'It's safe,' I said. 'For when it's needed.'

April Dawn smiled again. Some of the strain had gone out of her face.

'Why are you telling me all this?'

'Because you asked,' I said. 'You obviously had a reason.'

She nodded. 'I did. Trygon knew you had found out too much. So you had to be eliminated. But in a more subtle way. There

94

were too many bodies around already.'

'You're not talking about more truck drivers?' I said.

April Dawn started. 'You're sharp, Mike. Even Trygon would have to admit it. There were three in all, including Kovacs. And Trygon was worried in case the whole operation was uncovered. Things were all right until this new housing project. Alcazar Trucking had the biggest slice. And their dumpers passed close to here. Too close for Trygon's liking. He thought the first, certainly the second would discourage the truckies. But he was wrong.'

'How did he expect to get away with it?' I said. 'The police must have a lot of stuff on their files already.'

April Dawn shrugged. 'I told you he was mad.'

'But you haven't told me who he is and what's going on up the canyon that needs a passport control,' I said.

She laughed. It made a forlorn sound in the gloom tinted by the gold and red from the neons.

'That would be telling, Mike,' she said.

She tapped the small envelope she had taken from the bureau against the side of her face; the worried look was back in her eyes again. A small breeze from the open window rippled the curtains. I came closer to her. I held out my hand for the envelope but she put it behind her and shook her head.

'If we're not going any further then what's the point of this whole operation and you inviting me up here, April?' I asked.

She put out her hand to me and held my wrist; I caught that elusive perfume. The one that reminded me of the South of France and being young again. Only this wasn't the time either.

'Have patience, Mike,' she said. 'There is a point and you'll see it very soon.'

I put out my cigarette in an ashtray on the bedside table. She didn't let go my wrist but just stood and watched me gravely until I'd finished. I could feel her body trembling faintly, the feeling transmitted through her small, finely shaped hand.

'I'll go along,' I said.

April Dawn smiled. It was a fine thing to see. 'That's great, Mike,' she said. 'But first we've got some other unfinished business.'

She moved in closer to me and turned up her face and closed her eyes.

'That's great too,' I said.

She smiled again. She opened her eyes. 'You weren't doing anything special tonight?'

'I wasn't,' I corrected her. 'But I am now.'

She kissed me open-mouthed. Her hands tightened round the back of my neck and then her body was along mine and I was supporting her weight.

'God, you're strong, Mike,' she breathed

when we eventually came up for air.

'It isn't strength, it's a weakness,' I said. 'And one I'm particularly prone to.'

She bit my ear. 'You brute,' she said. 'You know very well what I meant.'

It seemed like we fell downwards a long way through the night. I reached out my hand and put out the bedside lamp. A soft glow came in through the half-open door of the living room and gave me just enough light to see what I had to do. Her gown was held by a silk cord in front but she already had it open. She was naked underneath. Somehow, I'd figured she would be. Tonight wasn't just an ordinary social visit.

Her figure was sensational. Her firm breasts were as cool as melons under my hands. Her nails cut into my back as she pulled me down into a melting pit of shadows with her. 'Be brutal, Mike,' she whimpered. 'I've waited a long time for this.'

'Me too,' I said. 'These sort of experiences don't usually come with the job.'

'Work, man, work,' she said urgently. She moaned once as I forced her head back. The action was so hot and hard I didn't even have time to take my clothes off. Her body was magnificent in its strength and silkiness; her skin seemed to burn against mine. I must have felt things were pretty important because she actually screamed as I took her and then we were through the climax and the storm and coming into harbour.

'I didn't know it could be like this, darling,' she panted, putting her hot face into my shoulder as she wriggled round into a more comfortable position.

'Nor did I, honey,' I said, though I was referring to the Smith-Wesson, whose bulk in the webbing holster was giving me hell where my left side was pressed up against the hard-bunched springs of the bed. April Dawn tightened her arms round my neck and her white teeth snapped again in mock-ferocity at the skin of my shoulder. She pulled me urgently down to her.

'More, Mike, more,' she said. 'The action's hardly begun.'

Her body trembled in my hands and my blood-count started rising again. So I suppose I shouldn't have blamed myself too much. There was something not quite right in her voice though the trembling of her body was real enough. I opened my eyes and saw she had her own wide open; they were fixed in blank terror over my shoulder. I pushed her away and rolled as a loud hiss scalded the nerves over the distant hum of traffic which percolated into the apartment.

Something long and silvery buried itself with a thudding smash into the padded bed-head. I rolled again and reached for the Smith-Wesson as a second steel dart scored splinters from a bureau before riveting itself angrily into the wallpaper. Then I was on the shadowy floor, still rolling, the revolver caught in the flapping fold of my jacket as April Dawn screamed and went on screaming.

Chapter Ten

Target Practice

1

The hiss came again as I landed on the floor with a thud and got in behind the bed. April Dawn went on screaming. The high, thin sound fretted at the nerves. I searched down the green and gold dazzle of the neon which came from between the gap in the drapes at the window of the apartment. The crack the third dart made had come before I'd stopped moving. The gent with the compressed air pistol which was firing the darts was good on reflexes but not so hot on his aim.

Which was just as well. The artist had to be somewhere on the balcony outside the window and the circumstances now favoured me. I had got the Smith-Wesson up on top of the bed coverlets and was in a good position for a snap shot. April Dawn had stopped screaming now and was making low moans of fright. I could see her huddled form in among the rumpled sheets. I kept my head down and crawled along to the end of the bed; it was a little lighter here but the neon dazzle wasn't so strong for my eyes and I would have to risk being seen.

There was a long silence. I could see the French doors leading to the balcony were slightly ajar; there was a gap of about two inches which was where our friend had been firing from. Presumably low down, in order to make himself as small a target as possible against the light. If he kept aiming through the gap, which would make his field of fire rather limited, I might jam the doors against his pistol if my rush were quick enough. I got down behind the bed again and thought things out. There were too many ifs about the set-up for my liking. This was too nice an evening to go out on a stretcher. Especially after the way it had begun.

There was still light in the sky so I waited until my eyes had become accustomed to it and searched farther down the long stretch of window. Unfortunately the drapes were too thick to see through. It had to be the gap in the French doors; unless the gunman was already making his escape along the balcony. I wormed my way up towards the head of the bed and carefully pulled a pillow down towards me. I crawled to the end of the bed and threw the pillow towards the half-open living room door.

There was another sharp hiss and the pillow altered course dramatically in mid-air; it folded up and flew over towards the far side of the bedroom scattering a fine mist of feathers. While it was doing this I went in a quick, low, scrabbling dive across the carpet and in through the living room door. Something tore a strip of carpet from near my heels and then I was through. I slammed the door and turned the key in the lock.

I got to the main door of the apartment, checked that it was still secured as April Dawn had left it. I turned off the light switches so that the whole apartment was in darkness. Then I went over to the windows facing the balcony in this room. I heard a muffled noise from the bedroom while I was doing this. I flattened mysell against the wall near the door and waited. I could hear April whimpering even at this distance. The bronze door-handle started turning. I pushed the Smith-Wesson up against the door panel and hesitated.

I could have chanced a shot through the door but the risks seemed to me unnecessary; I might miss and in any case the noise would bring the whole hotel down on us. In which case several people might get hurt. There were other ways. I waited a moment longer. The handle started turning again. I went across the living room unlatched the big window and quietly eased myself over the sill. I was on a black and white tiled balcony with Italian cane chairs scattered about. There was a dramatic splash of scarlet in the evening sky and the chains of light, from the traffic going through L.A. looked like a million dragonflies in the darkness.

But this was no time for poetry, I told myself. I gum-shoed over to the far side of the balcony, crouching low as I passed April Dawn's bedroom, and got in flat against the wall. I stood and watched the half-open bedroom window and waited. There was no sound but the muted roar of distant traffic. Apparently the little rumpus we'd made hadn't been heard. Or maybe the sound of a girl screaming was an everyday occurrence at the Park Plaza.

The drapes at the window hung like folds of metal in the still air. Then I heard a click from the bedroom beyond. April Dawn was quiet now. I guessed she had gotten over her attack of nerves. The click came again. The sound was too distinctive to be the door lock. It sounded like the steel dart artist was re-loading for another session. I wondered how many darts the gun held. It would be pretty important to know that when it came to the pinch. There was another long interval of silence.

Then I saw the curtains at the window move slightly when there was no wind. I followed them down with my eyes; there was a shadow down near the floor of the terrace. Something that looked like a projecting tube. I brought up the Smith-Wesson. The gun bucked in my hand and the powder stung my wrist. With the roar and the flash which momentarily lit the gloom of the balcony a long sliver of wood tore from the edge of the window frame. A dark and bulky shape rolled rapidly through the window and away behind the garden furniture. The hiss of compressed air sounded again and a steel dart spanged viciously off something a few feet from where I was crouching.

The shrill, high scream of a woman came from an open window farther down the apartments. The noise among the tables and cane chairs went on. I shifted position while the enemy was confused and ran parallel to the windows; I was very conscious that I was now silhouetted against the neon signs out front but the roof garden soon ended in a right angle and if the fancy shooter went round then he would be against the light.

I was hoping the noise of the Smith-Wesson might have been taken for a car backfire but it sounded like there were too many nervous ladies staying at the Park-Plaza to make that stick for long. I stopped where I was and wormed my way in between the anchored umbrellas back towards the wall of the suite facing the balcony. That way I got rid of the silhoutte effect.

I waited. A neon for Firestone Tyres was winking angrily in the background and this would make a shot difficult. First I had to have a target. And the way these boys operated it wouldn't be easy. The screaming in the hotel had stopped; all the walls which faced the terrace showed blank, lightless windows to the night. Then I heard a slithering; I got down on my belly and strained my eyes through the twilight of the roof-garden. Right down by the edge of the building where it turned at right-angles and disappeared along the terrace there was a hand with a long black pistol. It groped like a blind worm as the snout of the barrel turned this way and that.

I held my fire. I was waiting for an eye to come round the corner of the brickwork; then I saw the pale blur of someone's face, about a foot above the gun barrel. I threw a quick shot, saw the bullet strike sparks from the wall by the gunman's head. He screamed as brickdust and powdered cement temporarily blinded him. The pistol dropped with a clatter to the terrace as I got up and went in a run towards the end of the building. When I was halfway there a lean hand came round and scooped up the pistol.

I flattened myself into the wall and edged to the corner. There was blood on the bricks here and a few drops on the terrace. I lay down and put my head cautiously round the wall. The terrace only went on for another twenty yards and my man, doubled up, with one hand to his face, was running along the parapet, outlined against the sky-signs. Lights suddenly came on in two of the French doors behind me, facing the terrace. There came a mumble of voices.

I went across the tiling fast. The tall man holding his face heard me coming. He jumped down from the parapet, still with one hand up to his damaged eye. The barrel of the pistol started to rise. I pumped two shots off on the run. At first I thought I'd missed him. The barrel kept on coming up and the thin man hung suspended against the backdrop of the fiery neons. Then his hand came away from his eye and went to his throat. The gun barrel started dropping towards the ground again as his legs buckled. He seemed to fold quite suddenly, like his legs were on hinges; a pink froth of blood came out of his mouth. He ran a nervous hand along his collar.

The pistol hitting the tiles made a sharp snapping sound and then he was gone, falling over backwards across the low parapet, one hand flung up in black cut-out like a final salute. He went straight down into a Park-Plaza neon sign underneath and I heard the brittle tinkle of thousands of pieces of glass as he went through the ornamental canopy over the entrance lobby on to the concrete flooring. It was only then that I heard the shouts, the hurrying of feet and the roaring of the traffic in the night. I went over to the edge of the roof and looked down.

There was a jagged hole in the canopy and a black ring round a splash of steps as passers-by milled about. A few feet below me blue sparks hissed and exploded as the naked wires from the shattered sign short-circuited. I suddenly felt very tired. I picked up the compressed-air pistol with my handkerchief and ran back along the terrace. The pistol felt very heavy. I brushed past two women who had come out of the French windows. They went back inside with little shrieks of alarm. I got to the window of April Dawn's room just in time to see another dark shadow go away down the terrace very fast. I hadn't banked on two of them.

The shadow slid over the parapet where a fire-escape ladder jutted its iron shape above the edge. I heard the clang of feet descending the treads. I went back into April Dawn's suite as the first faint thin note of a siren started coming down the boulevard.

2

I put the Smith-Wesson back in the holster; there was still light spilling in from the half-open door. Everything was as I'd left it. Except for the rumpled sheets and the red stain that seemed to be everywhere. April Dawn lay half-in, half-out of the covers, her face contorted with pain. One arm was hooked above her head and locked on to the padded bed-head. Her eyes were wide open and unseeing. She was still alive because I could see the faint movements of her flanks as she fought for breath and a single bead of perspiration ran down her face. I fished around and got a pillow cover and tried to staunch the blood from the wound in her side. She didn't seem to recognize me or to know what I was doing.

'Take it easy,' I said. Though what good that did was debatable. She heard me, though. Somewhere through the splinters of pain my voice must have penetrated.

'Mike?' she said. Her voice was so low I had to bend right over and put my ear to her lips. Somewhere in back there was the murmur of voices. Something banged on the outer door of the suite. I had to move fast. But I couldn't leave. Not then.

'I didn't know, Mike,' April Dawn said. 'I didn't want it like this.'

'Sure,' I said. I tried to make her more comfortable. She had a spasm then and fought for breath until the pain had passed. She clutched my arm and held on to it as though her grip would prevent her from slipping over the edge of life.

'Trygon's helicopter,' she said. 'Leaving from the house. Tomorrow night. Be there. After dark.'

'The house in the canyon?' I said. 'Your house.'

She nodded. A faint smile came on to her face, faded away with her breath. 'Not my house,' she said.

She coughed once, stiffened and fell forward. I pushed her gently back on to the pillow. A small trickle of blood ran from the corner of her mouth. I wiped it away with the sheet and closed her eyes. I picked up the pistol and the brown envelope April had given me. The knocking on the door was louder now. I took one look around the room before crossing to the window. A shadow brushed the tiling as I got out on to the balcony. A woman screeched in the gloom as I scraped by. The terrace seemed to be full of guests in robes and pyjamas. I went down the balcony at a run, hoping I wouldn't trip against any low chairs. I found the fire escape ladder the other man had used earlier. There might be someone waiting at the bottom but I had to risk that.

I went down fast. My feet made a loud clatter on the treads. The ladder seemed to finish up in an alley near where I'd parked my car. I got to the last section and kicked down the remaining ten feet on the counterbalance to get me to the ground. It was shadowy in here and I stepped off and let the end of the fire escape slide back up, holding it to make as little noise as possible.

Something breathed in the warm darkness behind me I lashed out instinctively, heard a grunt; hands grabbed at my throat and then we were rolling over against the rough surface of a wall.

Chapter Eleven

Flak in the Afternoon

1

I put my fist into something soft. There was a strangled bellow. I dragged a portly form forward into the light. The lips were blue; I relaxed the grip of my hands round his throat.

'For God's sake hold it, Mr Faraday, or I won't be responsible,' said Cardinal Bishop. I let go of him and he sagged against the wall, catching his breath.

'Sorry about that, but it was understandable,' I said mildly.

There came shouts and confused murmurs from the roof terrace I'd left.

'We'd better blow,' said Bishop thickly, adjusting his neck-tie. 'I'll explain later.'

It was about the first sensible thing he'd said since I'd met him. He took me by the arm and steered me down the alley. My Buick was parked at the end, facing away from the Park-Plaza. I fell behind the wheel as another prowl car siren joined the growing chorus behind us. I put the pistol in the dash and locked it. I opened the envelope. It was filled with blank sheets of notepaper. I smiled.

Head lamp dazzle fell across the entrance of

the alley, passed on. I engaged the gear and we drew away from the building; I could see the police-car lights still converging as we turned the end of the block. I waited until we got well away before I spoke again; Bishop sat glumly, occasionally putting his hand to his throat. He licked his lips once or twice.

'How come you got my car?' I asked him at last.

He lit a cigarette before he replied. 'I followed you tonight,' he said. 'I figured there might be trouble. You were so long inside I went round in back and drove your heap out.'

He grinned suddenly, answering my unspoken question. 'I got a set of keys that operate most ignitions. I find it useful.'

'Why did you follow me?' I said.

'Just a hunch,' said Bishop. 'I get them sometimes.'

I shaved round behind a fruit truck and waited for him to go on.

'So I wait in the alley and then I hear shots. Presently someone lights out down the fire escape, going pretty fast.'

'You didn't try to stop him?' I asked.

Bishop's face was momentarily in shadow as he answered.

'I don't get paid for to get myself killed,' he said sourly. 'He was a big guy, over six feet, dressed in a dark sweater, dark trousers and sneakers. He looked like a professional. I let him go.'

'Then why the heroic stuff when I came down?' I said.

Bishop stammered as he answered. 'I figured it would be you. I was trying to get hold of your arm to tell you it was me when the side of the alley fell on me.'

I grinned. 'Well, thanks, anyway, Bishop,' I said. 'It seems I owe you something after all.'

I could see him contorting his face in the light of a passing drug-store.

'I told you we'd make a swell team,' he said.

'Well, don't press your luck too far,' I told him. 'Things are going to get rougher from here on in. Looks like I've got to crack this case within the next twenty-four hours or my face will be on the police wanted-folders.'

Bishop shot me a shrewd glance. His gold teeth glinted. 'I know a place not far from here where we can get a shot of the right stuff while we think things out,' he said.

2

A blue piano wove tangled splinters of sound into the semi-darkness of the bar. I sat in the booth and looked at Bishop over the rim of my glass. The bourbon tasted raw and smoky on my tongue. I called the waiter over and ordered another round of the same. The waiter was a tall, lean character with plastered-down black hair. He wore a black and white striped waistcoat and a fixed scowl. I reminded myself not to tip him. He came back with two grubby glasses and put them down on the oak table in front of us. They left wet rings on the wood as we lifted them.

'You haven't told me what happened yet,' Bishop said patiently.

'There were two of them,' I said. 'I got one, the other escaped past you. The first one got the girl. But not before she gave me a decent lead.'

Bishop gulped; his chins wobbled and he looked more like a pineapple than ever. He downed his glass with a spasmodic gesture.

'You sure you want me to go on?' I asked. 'The less you know the better.'

'I think you're right, Mr Faraday,' he said gloomily. 'I'm more suited to desk work than this stuff. What's the next move?'

'First I've got to get rid of my Buick,' I said. 'The police would pick me up within two hours once the news gets around. The woman in the Park-Plaza took my name when I came in. I'd no means of knowing how things would turn out or I'd have been John Doe. I'd best hire a car and sweat out the next twenty-four hours.'

I studied Bishop curiously. 'Just why did you pick on Tintoretto Canyon?' I said.

'Process of elimination,' he said. 'I tried four other places first.'

Bishop finished off the liquor in his glass.

'I'll sit this one out too—at my office,' he said. 'You know the number if you want to get hold of me.'

I nodded. I fished around in my wallet and paid for the drinks. I put the bills down on the zinc tray on the corner of the table; I left the smallest tip for Smiling Billy I could find in my pocket. He got the message all right. He shuffled over and picked up the tray.

'What's this?' he said nastily. 'Looks like I'm gonna need help to carry it.'

'And while you're at it,' Bishop told him, 'you and your friend can bring us two cups of coffee to finish up with.'

The coffee was coming as I went into a booth and dialled Stella's home number. It was one of the good evenings. She answered straight away. I filled her in on what had happened and asked her to take notes. I thought she'd raise some objections but she only asked me how to spell Trygon. Every time I thought I knew Stella some fresh facet came up to surprise me.

'Can't stay on long, honey,' I said. 'This call might be traced. I'll have to go underground for a couple of days, but I'll ring in. The big action is supposed to be tomorrow night at the Canyon. If you don't hear from me by midday the day after tomorrow ring Captain Dan Tucker and get that set-up investigated.'

I waited until I was sure Stella had everything down. She knew enough not to argue. I might only have a few hours and I had to disappear completely in that time. I glanced over towards Bishop. The coffees had arrived and even from here I could hear the argument going on with the waiter. Bishop seemed to be winning. I grinned and turned back to the phone.

'You will take care, Mike,' Stella was saying warningly.

'I seem to have heard that before,' I said.

She gave a cluck of disapproval that was echoed by the phone going back on its rest.

'You know I will, darling,' I said to the dead mouthpiece. I put the phone back on its cradle thoughtfully and went over to Bishop. He was sucking at the rim of a black and gold coffee cup, greedily scooping up the cream of the Vienna coffee with his thick lips. My dislike of him momentarily came back.

'We'd better blow, pretty quick,' I said.

'Sure, Mr Faraday,' he said, guzzling at the rim of his cup. 'I sure told that cheap tray pusher where he got off.'

We drank the coffee in silence. The dive was fairly empty but I spent the time studying the clientele. I could see no-one that resembled the man Bishop had described to me. Bishop called the waiter back and ordered a doughnut. He looked at me inquiringly as he shovelled the jammy mass inside his gold-toothed mouth. 'You think maybe I ought to go tell the police all about this set-up, Mr Faraday and let them handle it?' he said, returning to his old whining manner.

'Kiss the Mayor's Ass-Week begins on October 27th,' I told him. Bishop winced. A dull flush spread over his mottled cheeks. 'It was only an idea, Mr Faraday,' he said. 'I got my licence to think of.'

'Well, forget it,' I said. 'I'm the one sticking his neck out. You sit on your fat butt and be on that phone when you're needed and maybe we'll make out all right. You wanted this assignment, remember.'

'Sure,' said Bishop gloomily. 'I'm not likely to forget.'

I let that one go. It was around midnight when we left; we'd been inside the bar less than half an hour but I intended to circle the block just the same, before collecting the Buick. I reached for my pocket but Bishop stopped me.

'I'll pick up this tab,' he said. It must have been all of two dollars.

'Last of the big spenders,' I said.

'I don't do it for everyone,' Bishop said.

I figured he might make human being one day if he worked at it.

3

I made sure there was no-one around and got the Buick. Then I dropped Bishop off near his own part of town. He said he'd stand by until he heard from me. I drove off wondering how far I could trust him. He hadn't made out badly so far. I drove across town until I found an all-night garage where I wasn't known. I found a character in the glassed-in office in rear and booked the car in for a service under the name of Eldridge; the character in the office was bored and half-asleep and he didn't give the Buick more than a glance. He handed me a receipt for my deposit and I drove the Buick in under the echoing metal roof until I found a spot right down the end of an aisle where it couldn't be seen from the road. There were already over fifty cars in there and I figured it would take the police weeks to check every auto premises in the city. By which time I hoped to have an explanation that would stick. Or I might finish up leaving my name on three kills. I told the character I'd call for the car within a week and went on out.

I walked a couple of blocks to a drug-store and bought a razor, some soap and other toilet things and got the clerk to throw in a towel and put the whole lot in a plastic container. I couldn't go back to my rented house in Park West and it might be uncomfortable waiting for the following night. Then I got a cab across town to a car-hire firm that worked all round the clock. I rented a grey and black Cadillac that looked neutral enough to pass without comment, giving another phoney name.

The clerk on duty here was as tired-looking as the garage man and didn't insist on documentation. The look of my money must have convinced him of my honesty. I signed the insurance papers and the other stuff and a quarter of an hour later I had gassed up and was on the move again. Unless the tall man on the fire escape had been dogging me all the while I thought I had a pretty good chance of disappearing for the next forty-eight hours. I had hired the Caddy for a three-day period and I didn't want to leave a trail of fraud behind me as well as murder.

It was a quarter past one when I found a small motel nestling behind thick shrubbery. I made myself known, drove the Cadillac into the garage, dropped the door behind it and let myself into the apartment. Ten minutes later I was running a hot bath. By two a.m. I was diving into bed. I was asleep before my head hit the sack.

4

A scarlet Cessna was throbbing and spitting blue smoke out into the sunshine as I drove up to the small private airfield. The far hills looked blue and cool against the heat haze that was beginning to spread out in the distance. I'd rung Bill Swain before I'd had breakfast at the motel and told him what I wanted.

I parked the Caddy alongside a blue-painted metal hangar and walked across the concrete apron to an office building. A red windsock on a metal pole at one end of the field hung limply in the flaccid air. Somewhere a metallic voice was spitting instructions through a loud-speaker. Out on the parched grass near the outer perimeter of the field a small red and green low-wing monoplane was doing circuits and bumps. I stopped to watch for a minute. The pilot was even hitting the ground on purpose occasionally.

I went in through a glass door with AIR CONTROL stencilled on it. There was a long room with a floor of grey linoleum; maps covered in clear plastic occupied one wall and there was a powerful air to ground radio panel set at the end, two operators with ear-phones handling what traffic there was. Several men in flying clothes sat around in padded leather armchairs, reading magazines and looking like they were waiting for the Battle of Britain to break out. Bill Swain stood at one end of the room, near the big windows which faced the airfield and did something with a long pointer on one of the maps.

He looked up as I came in and waved cheerfully. He was a tall, lean man with a powerful body and shoulders thickly muscled; his hair was greying now and closely cropped to his skull. He'd had a hard time of it for some years but Swain Aviation was now established as one of the best and most efficient small charter outfits in this neck of the woods. But Bill had been a close personal friend for almost twenty years and could be relied on to keep his mouth shut; which was why I'd chosen him. I'd booked out the flight in the name of Bennett; Bill was going out on a limb doing me this favour and I hoped there wouldn't be any kickbacks from the police.

I'd checked through the Examiner carefully that morning; they'd made a fairly big downpage splash on the Park-Plaza shindig. To my surprise April Dawn had been referred to in the story merely as 'an unidentified blonde'; the classic newspaper cliché. The character who'd gone through the hotel canopy was a small-time mobster called Dillon who'd done three stretches for homicide; he'd been quiet for the past two years and I gathered the police weren't sorry to see the last of him. There was no mention of the third man on the roof or anything which pointed to my presence. Which didn't mean a thing, of course. The L.A. Police Department weren't likely to issue anything to the press which might put me on my guard.

'Can you hold on for ten minutes,' Swain called. I nodded and sat myself in the nearest armchair where I could watch the people in the room and at the same time see who was coming in the Air Control door. Swain went on talking to a stockily-built man in the uniform of a commercial airline pilot who stood beside him and watched Swain's pointer; they seemed to be beating their gums about wind-drift.

Whatever it was it seemed pretty fascinating as a topic. They finished at last and Swain came over. He gave me a hand like a steel gauntlet to shake.

'Come on in the office and sign the blood-chit,' he said. We went through into another long room painted cream; a blonde number with a figure that wasn't hard on the eyes sat and fooled with some air traffic blanks and pretended not to listen to the conversation.

'That will be all for the moment, Miss Ball,' said Swain mildly. 'I should wheel along to the canteen and get a cup of coffee if I were you.'

The blonde job got up with startling speed.

'Certainly, Mr Swain,' she said demurely. She looked wistfully at me over Swain's shoulder and gave me a deliberate wink. Her heels rat-tatted out over the linoleum. Swain grinned and waved me to a black leather chair near his desk. He was an ex-Army Air Corps pilot who'd been flying over the Hump on the Lashio-Chungking boneyard run during the war and he still had the Army stamp on him. He was the right man for the little jaunt I had in mind.

He leaned forward and took a cigar out of a box on the desk in front of him. He pushed the box towards me. I shook my head. Swain came up with another box full of cigarettes. I took one and lit up from the lighter he held towards me. Swain pierced the end of his cigar to his satisfaction and puffed out clouds of pungently scented blue smoke toward the ceiling. He leaned back in the chair, scooped up a document from his well-stacked blotter.

'Sign there,' he said. 'The usual disclaimer crap.' He hooded his eyes and stared out to where the Cessna was still spitting out fumes in the still afternoon air. A mechanic in white overalls went round in front of the whirling propellor and waved with his two hands to someone in the cabin. The throbbing of the motor died and the propeller blades became visible as the engine slowed to a crawl.

I signed the document Swain had given me. It said I made the trip at my own risk and absolved Swain from damages in case of injury or death. I initialled the other clauses about insurance where Swain indicated. I pushed back the paper when I'd finished.

'What's all this about, Mike?' Swain asked lazily.

'If I could tell you, I would, Bill,' I said. The big man looked at me curiously, opened his mouth as if to say something and then closed it again. He chewed on his cigar ruminatively.

'You know this could cost me my licence if the Civil Aeronautics Board got to hear of it,' he said, shaking his head. 'There are strict rules about things like this. Three hundred feet is plumb crazy up in those canyons. The air lanes are clearly laid down in regulations.'

'Since when did you take notice of the regulations,' I said.

Little pinpoints of light flared in Swain's eyes and his jaw tightened. Then he relaxed. He threw back his head and roared with laughter.

'That's true, Mike, and you're paying me well. But if anything does go wrong you better back me up.'

'How long have you known me, Bill?' I asked.

'Too long,' he said, smiling again. He raised his hand in protest as I pushed the bundle of notes over towards him.

'All right, Mike. All right. You made your point. I know I can rely on you. And half of that is what we agreed.'

He sorted the bills out and put the rest into my hand, closed my fingers around them.

'Leave everything to me. I made out a flight plan. You sign out in the name of Bennett, same as you signed the blood chit. That way we cover ourselves. And the girl doesn't know you.'

'A pity,' I said. 'She looked all right.'

Swain smiled again, almost regretfully. 'I'm getting a bit old for that,' he said, running his hands over his greying scalp.

'You'll be too old for that when they bury you,' I said. 'Not before.'

Swain got up, putting the notes in an inside pocket of his grey canvas windcheater.

'Maybe you're right, Mike,' he said. 'Maybe you're right.'

5

The cabin of the Cessna vibrated as Swain revved up the single engine. The radio spat static into the warmth of the small space. I sat in the co-pilot's seat next to Swain; the aerial camera I'd asked for was on one of the two seats behind us. The tower gave Swain permission to line-up. He looked into the sun, screwing up his eyes to see the answering pin-point of light from the controller. Then he released the brakes and we were lurching forward, off the apron and on to the grass of the field, hard now as concrete from the sun of the long, hot summer.

Swain taxied into the wind, his hands firm on the control wheel, his feet busy on the rudder. We waited for two or three minutes. A small Piper Apache went down a parallel course fifty yards or so away from us, flighted stiffly into the air. The light winked from the control tower again.

Swain released the brake once more and then we were gathering speed over the grass; a slight lurch, the Cessna seemed to side-step, Swain corrected and then he put the wheel forward, gently eased upwards and we were unstuck, the ground looking yellow now with the heat of the sun, climbing smoothly towards the north.

Swain handled the controls delicately, never

taking his eyes from the instrument panel until I could see the altimeter register 1,500 feet. Then he shot me a crooked grin.

'I'll make a leg,' he said. 'We'll fly on the V.O.R. beacon system. I'll approach Tintoretto from the north and we'll make a couple of runs. When we get among the hills I'll be able to drop down and carry out a box search. I hope you know what you're looking for.'

I didn't but I tried to look confident for Swain's benefit. It was nice like this, flying at about 3,000 feet with the blue ranges of the hills slipping slowly under the starboard wing-tip. The Cessna handled sweetly and Bill Swain nursed it along with an inbred instinct that marked the true professional. Word was around L.A. that he'd never lost a crewman during the war. I believed it.

'We got two and a half hours range,' Swain said. 'Plenty of time to do the job.'

I nodded. Swain leaned forward and turned the button on the V.O.R. dial. He read off the bezel which gave him a compass bearing for his first beacon. The needle on the dial, which deviated right and left, homed on to a series of beacons which pilots used both for day as well as night. He steered the aircraft until the needle indicated a true bearing for his next point. The Cessna flew sweetly on at about ninety-five knots. It was like being in a small saloon car and much more comfortable.

I tapped Swain on the shoulder. 'All right to

smoke?' He inclined his head. 'Sure, it's safe.'

I lit up and put my match stalk in a metal ashtray near the instrument panel. Swain chewed on the stump of his half-smoked cigar and glanced from the instruments down to the ground below and then back again.

He made his second turn about a quarter of an hour after we'd taken off. The high wings tilted against the sun as we went round, the bright light reflecting off the scarlet fuselage, and then Swain was re-setting the V.O.R. dial for the next beacon. We flew in this way for several minutes more. The character of the country had changed; far off to the south I could see the die-straight roads leading into the great industrial complex of L.A.; below us were low, parched hills crowned with thick vegetation and, winding in between, secondary roads that looped like snakes round the bases of the hills.

'We shall be hitting Tintoretto in about five minutes,' said Swain at last.

I reached in back to the rear passenger seats, undid the lap strap and fished out the big aerial camera; it had large steel handles and the simple mechanism, constructed to stand up to a lot of hard wear, operated the shutter to give a sharply detailed picture on roll film. The controls had been pre-set by Swain before we had taken off. I slid open the window at my side and rested the camera on the edge of the metal cabin door.

'Going down now,' said Swain. He tilted the wheel and the sky got up from where it was and went above us while the earth, the blue hills and the trees rotated slowly at the end of our spinning propellor. I leaned forward heavily in the straps retaining me to the padded seat and hoped I should be able to operate the camera properly when the time came. Swain tapped me on the shoulder as the scenery swung back to where it should have been. It seemed to me we were dangerously low. Trees and jagged outcrops of rock swung by high above us; below was a stream and several features were swimming into focus as we fled down a steep-sided valley, our shadow sharply etched on the ground by the brightness of the sun.

The engine rose to a high pitch as Swain opened the throttle and the Cessna staggered up; I saw the bare bones of a granite-edged ridge ride by seemingly only a few feet under the wing-tips and then the nose was pointing down again and we were floating over thick plantations of pine. Swain grinned at the expression on my face. He pointed downwards as he banked the aircraft steeply.

Then I saw it; the valley spread out below as sharply as an etching by Durer; white buildings that looked like a factory; toy figures strung out across a dazzling square as small as a pocket handkerchief; square blocks of metal that reflected back the sun blindingly. Swain put the aircraft round and then we were back, dropping down to 400 feet. I started operating the camera. Figures were running below us; a small group was waving from white steps in front of one of the concrete buildings; marching men dived in all directions as the engine of the Cessna beat heavily back from the ground.

A lorry lumbered its way across the concrete concourse as I began to take picture after picture; rolling the film on automatically, clicking the shutter, trying to keep the heavy body of the camera away from the soft vibration of the window edge. The Cessna skimmed in over a vast concrete dome and I could see more men running.

'Did you see that?' said Swain in disbelieving tones. 'They were tanks, man.'

He brought the aircraft skilfully round in a climbing turn, flattened out at the top and was then coming in again from the north. We must have made a black silhouette against the sun. I heard a crack and I saw Swain glance sharply at his instrument panel. The plane bucked and hot air seemed to suck at us. I glanced up out of the window and saw a black cloud of cotton wool floating level with us, about fifty yards away.

It drifted and dispersed just as another puff appeared in front of our windscreen. The aircraft jinked heavily as Swain handled the controls. He flew easily between the puffs of smoke which were now dotting the sky ahead of us. The noise ceased as we went down below the level of a ridge. The barrack block appeared again as I started to take pictures. The men on the ground had stopped running now.

Then there was a noise like a boy drawing a stick along a fence. A chain of bright sparks came tumbling slowly towards us. There was a bang and smoke came from a wing-tip; I looked to port and saw a series of small holes stitch themselves across the fabric of the aircraft.

'Christ!' Swain exploded, the reserve which had suspended disbelief for the last thirty seconds breaking at last. 'The crazy bastards are shooting at us!'

Chapter Twelve

Unhappy Landing

1

The cessna spun crazily for a few seconds, hung in the air with the motor screaming and then Swain had the machine under control again. The nose dropped, the full power of the engine sounded normally and we were rocketing over the trees and down the draw. I just had time to see the customs post at the end of Tintoretto Canyon flash past beneath the wing-tip and then we were flying straight and level with the engine throttled back as Swain grimly set course for the next beacon.

'Man, oh man,' he said over and over again between his teeth. I sat and thought up my story. Swain turned to look at me once he had got the aircraft on course; he kept shooting glances at the wing-tip. 'You knew all about this, Mike?'

'Only a hunch,' I told him. 'If I'd known what we were going into I'd never have booked the flight.'

Swain cautiously turned the wheel; we would soon be back over the field.

'God knows how I'm going to explain this to the Board,' he said gloomily.

'Say nothing,' I told him.

Little spots of red stood out on Swain's cheeks as he turned back to me.

'Are you crazy?' he said heatedly. 'You want me to lose my licence?'

'There are bigger things than licences,' I said. 'Take my advice. Get hold of a mechanic you can trust. Have that wing-tip patched up and leave the rest with me. In three days the whole business will be sorted out and you'll be in the clear.'

Swain shook his head warily like he'd heard it all before. 'I don't know, Mike,' he went on. 'That firing must have been heard clear to L.A.'

'Thunder,' I said. 'Or a film company doing location work for a war film. You know California.'

Swain shook his head again. 'Perhaps you're right. But if you can get away with this it beats all. Why the hell would anyone want to shoot at a low-flying aircraft over this sort of real estate?'

'All shall be revealed in the last reel,' I said.

Swain's eyes glinted. He set the Cessna down light as an angel-cake just over the boundary of the field. The hangars of the installation started coming up in the middle distance.

He broke into harsh laughter. 'Well, it'd better be a good explanation, Mike,' he said. 'The Lashio run's one thing in war-time, this is another. It had sure better be good.'

'It will be, Bill,' I said. 'It will be.'

Swain taxied the Cessna up to the concrete apron in front of the hangars and cut the motor. I noticed the damaged wing-tip was on the side away from the office windows. A sandy-haired mechanic with a lop-sided grin came out of the hangar whistling. He went round the aircraft. He glanced up at the port wing-tip and stopped whistling. His jaw trembled for a moment and he looked towards Swain. Then he regained his sang-froid. He poked his face in the cabin door as Swain opened it.

'They got big woodpeckers up in them thar hills,' he told Swain laconically. The pilot scowled. He got down from the cabin and took the mechanic by the arm. They went off a ways and I could see them arguing through the scratched plexiglass of the cabin window. I unstrapped myself, got out my side of the aircraft and dropped to the concrete. I walked towards Swain.

'All right,' he said heavily. 'We'll play ball. Three days, like you said.'

'Thanks, Bill,' I said. 'And if anyone comes around asking for me, the name was Bennett.'

Swain lifted his cigar butt and belched heavy clouds of blue smoke towards the blue sky.

'Sure, Mike, sure,' he said, screwing up his eyes against the sun.

The sandy-haired mechanic came up from the hangars; he strapped a length of sacking round the damaged wing-tip as another mechanic in white overalls strolled across the grass towards us. Swain shook hands briefly and then he and the two mechanics started pushing the Cessna round behind the hangars. I lit a cigarette and went on over towards the spot where I'd parked the Caddy.

I was halfway when I saw a big blue prowl car of the L.A. police roll up towards the office building. I put on a pair of dark glasses I had in my breast pocket and got behind the wheel of the Caddy fast. I slumped down in the driving seat and watched the prowl car glide to a halt.

Two men in plain-clothes got out, while a third, in uniform, remained at the wheel. The two men went on into the office, walking with fast, purposeful steps. I hoped Swain would know what to say. I quietly let in the gear and rolled out through the airfield gates. I saw the police car in my rear mirror but the driver didn't move and no-one came out the office. I got into the traffic and drove off fast across town.

2

I drew up in rear of a cheap diner in an obscure part of town and got outside their blue-plate special. I finished the cold beer and ordered another. While I was waiting for it to come I went into the pay-booth at the end of the long, shabby dining room and rang the office. I looked carefully round as I dialled. There were only two or three other people in the place and the waiters were like walking zombies but I made my living dealing with the unexpected. Stella answered.

'This is Mr. Bennett,' I said, like we'd arranged.

'Yes, Mr Bennett,' said Stella. 'I was expecting your call. McGiver was here about an hour ago.'

'Thanks,' I said. 'They were at the airfield too.'

Stella sounded worried. 'Are you all right for money and transport?'

'Yes to both questions,' I told her. 'Listen carefully. I haven't got much time. If I catch too much trouble get on to Tucker and blow everything. Bishop is standing by so keep him informed. He's been surprisingly useful.'

I gave Stella the details and waited while she took notes.

'This is the important stuff,' I said. 'The villa up at Tintoretto is being used as a front. The valley beyond is stiff with tanks and other equipment and men dressed like regular troops. Why, I don't yet know. Someone called Trygon's in back of it. There's a helicopter leaving from the house tonight after dark. Presumably for what's up the canyon. I aim to be on it. Give me twenty-four hours after ten tonight to be on the safe side. If you don't hear by then get Tucker in.'

'Check,' said Stella. There was a slight pause.

'Good luck, Mr Bennett,' she said.

'Thanks,' I said softly and meant it. There was a click as the receiver at her end went down. I got out the booth, drank my beer, paid the check and left. There was no-one around when I got back in the Caddy. I drove to a quiet place to sweat it out until dark.

3

I extinguished my fifth cigarette and looked at my watch for the hundredth time in the last two hours. I felt the bulk of the Smith-Wesson in its webbing harness against my chest; I'd used four slugs on the man on April Dawn's balcony. I had a spare clip and I'd re-loaded; the Smith-Wesson held five so I had one spare at the bottom of the holster. I hoped it would be enough for what I wanted to do. But what did I want to do? I went over again April's crazy dialogue about the mad Trygon.

It was now past ten. A car with two men in it had driven up just before dark but I hadn't been able to see clearly who was in it. The porch lights had been extinguished and the front door was at the other side of the house anyway; I was somewhere up Tintoretto Canyon near my old position where someone had taken a shot at me. I figured it was as good a place as any; I'd put the Caddy in the same layby I'd used when I had the Buick.

There were a few lights showing from the house but nothing like exceptional activity which would have indicated something special going on. There was always the possibility that April Dawn had been lying but in my experience dying people don't lie as a rule and April had known she was going right enough. I sat down with my back to a tree and looked up at the sky; it was a fine clear night with plenty of stars showing. Then, suddenly, the balance of light in the sky changed. I stood up and saw the whole of the garden area at the back of the house below was luminescent. Powerful floods suspended on thick cables were strung from trees and along an ornamental pergola that fringed the lake. I heard the characteristic chopping roar in the sky and then the brighter stars were blotted out as something passed across them.

The navigation lights of the helicopter looked like fierce jewels as the machine hovered over the lawns of the house; the lights went out and then came up again almost instantaneously. Figures started coming out of the house as I went down the hillside at a run, oblivious of any noise I might be making. In the brief space before the lights finally died I saw that the big Sikorski helicopter bore the standard markings of the L.A. Police Department.

Two pale oblongs of light spilled out of the French windows facing the terrace and made long slivers of orange across the still surface of the lake. I could hear the murmur of voices over the water as I got among the trees. I had the Smith-Wesson out and felt confident of being able to deal with any sentries who might be posted. But somehow I didn't think they'd be keeping a very careful watch on this side of the house tonight.

When I came out of the belt of trees I was only a few hundred yards away from the house with the Chinese gateway; I found out later it was an appropriate symbol. The rotor blades of the helicopter had stopped turning and two men, presumably the crew, were up on the terrace with a small group of people who were standing around in front of the house. There wasn't much light at the far side of the lawn where the machine was parked, about a hundred yards from the nearest trees but it looked like a long way from where I was standing and if someone threw the light switch when I was halfway across I'd be a sitting target.

I went on over anyway. There wasn't anyone near the machine and I crept up underneath its belly; I got down on my knees behind one of the big wheels and looked over towards the terrace. The group seemed to be dissolving away and one or two people had gone back inside the house. There came the faint murmur of voices. There was a metal ladder reaching down from the body of the helicopter and making a slatted pattern against the glow from the terrace windows. I was standing right behind it; I hesitated for a moment.

There might still be someone left inside the helicopter but I didn't think so. I ran back a few yards and scooped up a handful of gravel from near the edge of the lake. I flicked a small piece up towards the perspex blister of the front cabin; it made an audible click easily discernible to anyone inside but it would not have been heard from the terrace. There was no response so I repeated the gesture with the same result.

Five minutes had passed and I should have to get moving if I wanted to be in on the action. I looked back at the house. There were three people still standing talking just outside one of the French doors. All three had their backs turned to me and were conversing in turn with a fourth person who was inside the house. I got up the metal ladder feeling that dozens of eyes must be watching me; I stumbled cautiously into the dark interior of the machine, felt the padded leather of seats.

The interior smelt of gasoline, cigar smoke and leather, in that order. The three men were still on the terrace but as I looked down towards them they disappeared into the house. I went slowly down an aisle between the seats of the small cabin, adjusting my eyes to the gloom in there. Presently I found some crates stacked in rear. They were about four feet high and by pushing them forward a little I found I could just crouch uncomfortably behind them without being seen from the cabin seats, which faced away from me up towards the pilot's blister. The crates were heavy and took some shifting without noise; from the faint light which came through the sliding hatch of the machine I could see, according to the stencilled lettering, that they contained spare machine parts. I sat down behind the crates to wait.

More than half an hour must have gone by before I heard noises from outside, followed by muffled conversation. Then there was the clang of feet on the metal treads of the ladder. A fumbling about in the interior of the machine followed; a pale blue light went on and I could hear two men talking. I eased up a little and got my eye to a space between two crates. The men appeared to be the pilot and co-pilot of the machine but apart from their dark military-style uniforms the glance told me nothing. The two men were leaning over the seats in front of their instrument panel and were checking off the dials. There was a slight argument going on which was presently clinched by the pilot saying he was satisfied with the readings.

Then followed the scratching of matches on a rough surface and the two men smoked as they sat in the padded leather chairs in front of the control panel. Another long wait ensued; then I heard a buzz. The pilot lifted a receiver from its cradle and listened for a few moments. Bright lights shone in the interior of the machine. At the same time footsteps sounded on gravel and the sound of many voices came towards the helicopter. I crouched down behind my crates and tried to make myself as small as possible. I had laid the

Smith-Wesson on the floor as it was beginning to cramp the muscles of my hand but it was where I could get hold of it if I needed it in a hurry.

And that might be soon. I risked a quick glance through the crack as more footsteps sounded on the ladder. The pilot and co-pilot had their peaked caps on; they were standing at attention and saluting towards the doorway. Two small men with dark oiled hair came into the cabin; they wore light fawn overcoats and carried leather briefcases chained to their wrists. They were accompanied by three or four other men, one at least of whom was dressed in some sort of military uniform. The two small men listened impassively as the former went on speaking. 'Certainly, Mr Pen Ching,' he was saying. 'The President was most emphatic upon that point.'

The lights in the cabin went out soon after and what further conversation there might have been was drowned in the roar of the engine. Only the blue ceiling lights remained. I put my head up briefly again and saw that the six or seven men in the big cabin had strapped themselves into their seats. The pilot was saying something inaudible into the intercom he held in his hand. Someone hauled up the metal ladder and a few moments later the sliding door closed and was secured.

Dazzling light shone through the cabin windows from the ground; the shuddering roar increased and then the note changed and we were hovering, the engine turning the great rotor blades faster. They were biting the air and we were lifting smoothly and fast, the dark tops of trees falling away below us and then the lights were extinguished and we were suspended in the dark. We kept on going up and in the distance I could see the faint glare and haze that marked the farthest perimeter of L.A., before the hills and the canyons took over from the neon-lined boulevards.

I lay and flexed my jaw to get rid of the heavy feeling in my eardrums as the Sikorski banked and the horizon fell far below until there was nothing but the glow of the instrument panel and the overhead lights in the darkness and out through the windows the distant pinpoints of the unfriendly stars. We flew up the canyon, occasionally circling and hovering, for about twenty minutes, until I could see more lights from below, reflected on the tree-tops.

I could hear the pilot talking on the intercom and presently we began to come down. There was an almost imperceptible jolt and then the motors cut and the only noise remaining was the hissing as the great blades continued to rotate and chop the air at ever diminishing speed. I kept lying there, hoping they wouldn't unload the crates, until the noise of feet and voices had ceased. When I judged the cabin was clear I looked up and saw that the pilot was still at the instrument panel. He was tapping one of the dials and swearing to himself. Presently he got tired of this and then he went away too.

When I judged it was safe I got to my feet, stretched and put the revolver back in my shoulder holster. I had got halfway down the empty cabin and up towards the door when it was suddenly slid to from the outside. I got down behind one of the leather seats in nought seconds flat. Whoever had moved the door hadn't fully shut it and I could still see through a gap of about eighteen inches.

The machine started to move while I was thinking about this. Light blossomed outside the front cabin windows. There was a hangar up ahead, with bare electric bulbs lighting the white concrete walls and the stark functional lines of the steel girdering which held up the roof. A cable had been attached to the nose of the helicopter and it was slowly being winched into the hangar. I could hear the faint hum of a motor. One or two men in black coveralls stood around and watched silently.

I put my head down and lay with my face to the floor as the machine came in under the bright lights. Presently the noise of the winch stopped and I could hear the cable being unshackled from the nose of the machine.

There was another long silence and the lights in the hangar went out. I gave them another half hour and then I got up. There wasn't a sound anywhere and only a single red light burning up near the hangar entrance disturbed the darkness. I got through the helicopter door, hooked my hands over the edge and dropped quietly to the concrete floor. The high fret of a pump working sounded from far away. Keeping in the darkest shadow I went up towards the hangar entrance. It was a pity about the red light but things had gone my way so far and I decided to risk it.

I had got out the Smith-Wesson again and holding it before me slipped under the lamp and into the darkness beyond; I was perhaps a second, maybe a fraction less, but it was enough for someone. The top of my head exploded in blinding light. What a hell of a way to make a living I thought to myself as I went spiralling down into an ever deeper darkness.

Chapter Thirteen

A Summons from the President

1

Moments of agony long drawn out. A diamond shape forming and dissolving in front of my eyes. Noise that ebbed and flowed harshly. Noise that presently resolved itself into voices.

'You didn't hit him hard enough, Usher,' said someone.

A harsher, stronger voice replied. 'He'll do. If I'd meant him to stay hit I wouldn't have missed. The President will want to interrogate him.'

The other man laughed. 'For how long? So you've extended his life by three hours or so. How important is that?'

'Pretty important to him, I guess,' said the man called Usher easily.

The first man laughed again. I lay picking the pieces together and trying to make an intelligible conversation in my mind. The sense of what they were saying seemed to lag a long way behind the sentences. I thought for a moment of the undeveloped aerial shots which were locked in the dashboard cubby of the Caddy back in the layby. I should have passed them over to Stella before I came on this trip. But it was too late to think of that now. Almost too late for anything.

I closed my eyes and rolled over. When I opened them again I could see the whorled surface of concrete close to my face and it was properly in focus. The woolliness went away from my brain but my head throbbed like a diesel engine. I moved my hand across the rough surface of the floor. I knew the Smith-Wesson had gone and I found my pockets had been turned out too. An expert had given me a real going over.

I turned and looked upwards. The waves of nausea had passed and I could see clearly. I was in a small room with a concrete floor and concrete walls. There were two barred windows set high up and a metal door. Bare bulbs burned in three metal fittings in the white-painted ceiling. The man called Usher was very tall and thin, but with broad shoulders and a useful ripple of muscle under the polo-necked blue sweater he wore. He had bright blue eyes, a tough, friendly face and a thin white scar ran from the corner of his left eye almost to his chin.

The man with him was aged about forty, with black, greasy hair and a thin mustache which ran arrow-straight under his nostrils; I would have bet that it wasn't a millimetre out of true either way. He had a big bulky body to go with his fat head and though he looked out of trim I should have said he was hard and fit despite his bulk. He was the sort who used a telephone directory for a handkerchief. He was dressed in a dark blue uniform with gold bars across the sleeves; there were decorations that jingled across his chest as he moved his arms, and a blued-steel revolver in a canvas holster buckled round his waist.

'You take too material a view of life, Smithers,' said Usher. 'Look at our friend here, for instance. I'll bet he's thinking of a way out of his situation right now.'

Smithers put a fat tongue across his lips and

144

shot venomous glance at me from the corners of his eyes.

'I daresay,' he said drily. 'You have a curious, not to say dangerous sense of humour, Usher. Particularly for the new Leader of No 1 Liquidation Group. I have ofter had occasion to speak to the President about it.'

'No doubt,' said Usher affably, without taking his eyes off me. He held the black-barrelled machine pistol almost affectionately in his right hand and had it resting across his knee. His right foot was up on an oak bench so that he leaned forward, half stooping, as he listened to Smithers' reponses. His legs were encased in brown leather riding boots which had a high polish. He glanced up towards the portly officer while his hand continued to wave the barrel of the pistol gently through the hundred and fifth degrees of an arc. It just took in the portion of the room in which I was lying.

'We'll get along fine as long as you remember two things,' said Usher, turning his bright blue eyes in my direction. 'Just leave the action to me and stick to the politics, Smithers.'

The fat man's pupils smouldered and he drew himself up. 'General Smithers, if you please,' he said. 'I have already had reason to comment on your laxity in these matters.'

He dropped his hand casually to the revolver butt at his waist.

Usher smiled but his face had gone hard. He wave the machine pistol in a wide circle.

'By all means, General, let us observe protocol.' He bowed ironically towards the other.

Smithers relaxed slowly. 'That is better, Usher,' he said gently. 'Decidedly better.'

'Colonel Usher, as long as we're being formal,' said the tall man and the smile had gone from his face.

Smithers' own features began to turn pink. He made a strangled grunt in his throat. 'I have better things to do than to stand here bickering with you all day,' he said furiously. He strode out of the room and slammed the door behind him. Usher's sardonic laughter sounded like the echo of the slamming door.

Then he turned slowly to me. His blue eyes were curiously metallic and quite devoid of feeling. The scar on his cheek stood out a dead white as he said in a low voice, 'You'd best get up now, Mr Faraday. Even our outfit doesn't like having to hold a man up to shoot him.'

2

I drank the coffee Usher handed me and felt better. I finished the cup and put it down on the bench at the side of the room. Usher refilled it in silence from a polished steel pot at his elbow. Two big men in blue uniforms stood impassively each side of the door. They held naked revolvers in their hands and they looked like they knew how to score ten out of ten for marksmanship. I glanced over at the pile of my stuff on top of the bench. The Smith-Wesson was there, together with my documents and other personal possessions. I wished, not for the first time, that I'd left my identification home. I seemed to have missed out on quite a few elementary things tonight. I saw that the revolver had been unloaded; all five slugs and the spare were on the table. Usher smiled slightly as he saw my glance.

He held up his watch, frowned at the dial and shook it to see if it was still going.

'Take your time,' he said softly. 'We're not due in the Conference Chamber for another hour yet.'

I finished the coffee and sat down on a long seat which ran in front of the bench. The hammers in my head had stopped playing the Star-Spangled Banner. I began to size up the situation. I hadn't yet seen anything of the organization here and I didn't know whether it was a question of dealing with half a dozen people or a couple of hundred. But if I hadn't been flown out of the Tintoretto Canyon base while I was unconscious, then there didn't seem much chance, remembering the plane trip I'd taken with Bill Swain.

Usher glanced over at me like he knew what I was thinking. 'It was you in the Cessna this morning?' he said. I looked down at the toes of my shoes and said nothing.

'He was a pretty good pilot,' said Usher admiringly. 'The way he dodged that flak. I've been expecting something like this. I tried to tell Trygon the whole thing would blow open one day but he never listens.'

'Perhaps he's got Hitler's intuition,' I said.

Usher chuckled. 'That's the spirit, buddyboy. You're real professional.'

There was something not unlikeable about Usher. Any other time, any other place I should like to have had him on my side; except that he'd gotten lined up with the wrong people. Whoever they were. With every minute that was passing my head was clearing. There came a knock at the door. One of the guards opened it. He called Usher over. The tall man disappeared into the corridor and I could hear a muffled conversation. He came back soon after. 'Looks like I'm wanted buddyboy,' he said, with a twisted smile. 'But don't worry. I'll be seeing you.'

He turned to the two men in military uniform at the door. 'Look after him,' he said sharply. 'Mr Faraday is a dangerous man.'

He glanced back to me. 'You see, Mr Faraday, you are something of a celebrity in this part of the world. And we don't take chances with celebrities.'

'Thanks,' I said. 'You might leave me some cigarettes.'

Usher extended his hand to the pile of my

stuff on the bench. 'Help yourself,' he said.

One of the guards came up quickly and removed the Smith-Wesson and the ammunition; he put it down on a small table over by the door. I sat down on the wooden settle and lit up as Usher went on out. I hadn't asked him for a blindfold but I felt like it.

3

It was over half an hour before Usher came back. The two guards snapped to attention as he came in the door. He was wearing a dark brown military uniform with a pistol in a black holster buckled in at his waist. There was a lot of scrambled egg on the edge of his military cap and again on his shoulders. He wore a silver cord with tassels looped across his chest and through the epaulette on his left shoulder. His shoulder flashes bore the legend; No. 1 Liquidation Unit, 4th Commando. Usher smoked a cigarette through a long jade holder and his blue eyes had a glint of humour as he glanced at me.

'Time to be moving,' he said crisply.

'I thought that stuff went out with Erich von Stroheim,' I said, giving his get-up the once-over.

Usher didn't change expression. 'It impresses the natives,' he drawled, flicking ash from his cigarette end over the floor. 'And of course the money's good.'

'Somehow I thought it would be,' I told him.

I got up as the two guards fell in on either side of me. 'If you'd told me this was to be formal I'd have brought my tuxedo,' I said. 'I don't feel I'm really dressed to meet the President.'

Usher looked me up and down. I could feel crusted blood on my forehead where he had dropped me in the hangar.

'I shouldn't worry about that, Mr Faraday,' Usher said. 'Our President's surprisingly informal.'

We went through the low door and into a steel-lined corridor which seemed to stretch an interminable distance; bulbs in round frosted globes spanned the run of the corridor. Usher walked level with me and the two guards about six feet in rear. Too far back for me to try anything. Not that I was likely to. I was far too interested in who and what President Trygon might be. I flexed my arms without making too much movement, as I walked I seemed to be all in one piece; I certainly felt more like tackling anything that might present itself.

Another guard in blue unlocked a steel door at the end of the corridor. Usher and my two guards waited until the door was re-locked behind us before they moved on. The tall man opened a metal box bolted to the wall of the short passage in which we were now standing. He took out a black telephone.

'Colonel Usher. Party for the Presidential Suite. Four persons. Conference Chamber.'

He listened quietly, thanked someone and put the phone back on its cradle. He closed the box. The four of us went down the corridor a short way and were then brought up by a gleaming metal wall. Usher pressed a buzzer set at the side of the corridor. It was evidently a pre-arranged code signal. With a barely audible rumble the steel wall slid back. Two enormous men with impassive faces stood inside the small square box which faced us. The overhead neon tube shone softly on their dark blue uniforms which had minute white skull and crossbone insignia on the lapels. Shone too on the blued steel snouts of the sub-machine guns they each cradled in their arms.

We went into the box, crushed together in the confined space, the door slid to behind us and we were whining upwards in the steel elevator towards the unknown pleasures of President Trygon's Conference Chamber.

Chapter Fourteen

Cabinet Re-Shuffle

1

There was a guard of honour lined up outside when the elevator whined to a halt. Twelve men in the blue uniforms which were becoming familiar, tommy-guns at the ready and wearing steel helmets. They looked like Filipinos from their features. This corridor was lined in panelled woods and was lit by crystal chandeliers. A rose-pink carpet stretched the length of the passage, which was all of a hundred yards.

I walked slowly down the middle with Usher at my side and the original guards keeping pace behind. Far in rear I could hear military orders being snapped out. Turning my head I could see that the twelve guards had formed up in a solid phalanx to cut off our retreat and were marching in slow order behind us. Usher stayed close to me. His face was grim and unsmiling.

When we reached the end of the passage two men dressed as junior officers took over from the two guarding me. The latter remained outside the heavy oak door which was our destination. With Usher leading and the new escort behind we went on through over a marble inlaid floor into the Conference Chamber. Remembering the lay-out from the air I was expecting something grandiose but this was fantastic. The room was about two hundred feet long, the far end being circular and the walls seemed to be made of metal. Diffused lighting came from concealed fixtures in the ceiling high above; there were big maps and diagrams set along the wall on our left, together with long blackboards covered with chalked data.

Our feet echoed hollowly on the marble as our party of four went across it. It seemed like a long walk to the far end where all the action was taking place. There was a horse-shoe table in walnut with six or seven men sitting around it; they all had blotters and pen-sets in front of them and most of them brief-cases at their elbows. It looked like an M.G.M. set for the Pentagon. There seemed to be an argument going on. The delegates or whoever they were spoke into miniature microphones in front of them and their conversation was relayed through speakers to a platform set in the open U of the table.

General Smithers came up with a worried expression as we marched down the room and met us halfway between the table and the door. He took Usher aside and the two men spoke in low tones. Usher came back.

'Detail follow me,' he said crisply to my

escort. The four of us altered direction and made for an enclosure created by the angle of two walls meeting at one side of the huge chamber. Usher pressed me down into a padded leather chair while the two officers came up behind me; I felt the chill of their pistols on the back of my neck. I was facing the horse-shoe table so I could see everything that was going on.

'But, Mr President,' a fat man was bellowing, 'this policy is liable to endanger everything this state stands for.' He hammered on the table with an ash-tray, he was so agitated. There was a murmur of assent from several others around the table. The figure on the dais facing the horse-shoe snapped his fingers; the click seemed to echo throughout the vast room and General Smithers hurried over as though someone had lit a fire under him. His boots made a metallic noise over the marble floor. The plump general bowed at the foot of the dais and listened quietly to the whispered instructions he was given. The men at the table waited impatiently.

'Yes, Mr President!' Smithers tore off the figure on the dais a West Point salute and went clattering back towards us. He passed by, his head held high and went out through the main door.

I sat and tried to forget the two circlets of chilled steel pressing into my neck. President Trygon was a remarkable sight by any standards. He sat in a vast arm-chair of black leather which was surrounded by metal levers projecting from a console built to one side and partly in front of his chair. He was a heavy, thickset man in an elaborate green and gold uniform bearing rows of medal ribbons and various kinds of whipped cream on its extremities. His face was broad as the moon, pink and hairless and his great bald scalp was like a reflection of his face. His mouth was a remorseless gap in his features. His eyebrows were thick and sandy and surmounted deep-set eye-sockets. His left eye was covered by an eyepatch made of some silver material which caught the light.

His one remaining eye, which was red-rimmed and bloodshot, had a gold monocle screwed into it; the thin gold chain of the monocle was secured to the third button of his uniform. He was around sixty, I should have said, and looked like he was used to giving commands and having them obeyed. He had a full-dress uniform cap with a red skull and crossbone badge on the front of it, lying on the console top at his side and something that looked like a gold-tipped field marshal's baton was held between the podgy fingers of his left hand. He twirled it by its leather strap as he addressed the meeting.

He had a silver whistle tucked through an epaulette and held against his shirt front by a white lanyard; and a pair of lavender gloves were folded and held by the black leather belt braced around his middle. For a minute, apart from his eyes and the lack of hair, I thought Hermann Goering had come back to life. The drift of his remarks concerned discipline and the welfare of the state; he was to be the sole arbiter in these matters and the men gathered there, his ministers and advisers, were to consider themselves fortunate that they had such a leader to guide them.

'I trust I make myself perfectly clear, gentlemen?' he said gently. The quiet, self-assured voice carried to every corner of the vast hall, and the effect of his trite words was electric.

There was a hesitant silence before the men assembled around the table returned to the attack. One who appeared to be their leader, a tall, thin man with a shock of blue-rinsed hair that fell almost to his shoulders, waved his papers about violently.

'The state cannot be maintained, Mr President,' he shouted excitedly. 'It is precisely because of this that an extraordinary Cabinet meeting has been called. With the incidents on the borders, then the aerial reconnaissance, it is surely only a matter of time before our existence is discovered . . .'

The President turned his one eye behind the gold monocle on the speaker, whose words trailed away falteringly into the air. Somewhere from far off the throbbing of the air-conditioning system sounded menacingly through the charged atmosphere.

'I am the President,' Trygon said emphatically, enunciating every syllable with precise clarity. 'I give the orders. The orders are to be obeyed. Your place is to do so without question. Twice in recent weeks my orders have been questioned. That cannot be tolerated.'

I saw General Smithers start to retreat rapidly to the side of the hall. He backed over towards our table. At the same moment Trygon started manipulating the metal levers in front of him. There was a muffled clang as a shining sheet shimmered from floor to ceiling between him and the men behind the horse-shoe table. The tall man with blue-rinsed hair reached inside his coat. He came up blasting with an automatic. The two shots sounded high and thin in the hall. The bullets smashed bright stars against the armoured glass surrounding the President.

He pressed more buttons on his console. The whole of his chair and the circular base underneath started to revolve; small louvred slits appeared in the metal surround. Trygon smiled as he pulled another lever. Flame and smoke spat from the holes; the noise was like a boy rattling a stick loudly over metal railings. Another sheet of bullet-proof glass slammed to the floor behind the U-shaped table, cutting off the Cabinet's retreat. A chair flew to

157

splinters as the President raked the room; I saw a fat man crouching behind the chair trying to ward off death with his naked hands.

One man ran up on top of the table in an effort to get to the President. He didn't make it; his body stiffened as blue smoke enveloped him. Trygon stitched him up; he twisted awkwardly and fell, his hands clutching at the air. Little flames came out the back of his suit, the cloth smouldering. He sagged downwards on to his face. Screams and yells came up shrill above the high-powered popping of the machine guns. Trygon's eyes were bright with malice as he kept on operating the buttons and levers; the whole of his chair up on the dias was wreathed in blue smoke with vicious little spurts of flame lancing from it, as he went to and fro in a fixed arc, like a war-time bomber's turret gunner.

I saw Smithers get down on his knees in front of us and cover his face. Presently the cries of the men inside the glassed-in chamber stopped; there were left only twitching heaps from which streams of dark crimson ran sluggishly. But still Trygon kept on firing until the splintered stars on the inside of the bullet-proof glass seemed to cover the whole of our vision like squashed flies on a car windscreen during a long journey in hot weather.

At length his revolving turret came to a stop and he gave his shining levers a last twirl with a flourish of satisfaction. Smithers got shakily to his feet in front of me and saluted Trygon stiffly to demonstrate his loyalty. The armoured glass shutters rumbled aside as we all got to our feet. I looked at Usher's impassive face.

'So that's what they call a Cabinet re-shuffle,' I told him.

2

The President lit a cigarette from a silver and crystal lighter on the console top at his side. He pressed a button and the oak doors at the far end of the Conference Chamber opened. The two officers with me hadn't moved; I could still feel the cold ends of their gun-barrels on my neck. The twelve men in blue uniforms who had been outside the entrance filed in. Orders snapped in the warm air. Stretchers were brought up and the bodies of the seven men were taken off; one of them was still alive. An officer crushed the man's skull with his revolver butt.

Another squad of men in white coveralls followed on; they started mopping the floor with long-handled mops and hot water. Two new chairs were brought in to replace those damaged. Another officer in blue took all the brief-cases and papers out for sorting. In less than ten minutes no trace of the massacre remained. The officer in charge of the detail, a square-jawed man with a black mustache saluted Trygon and stood respectfully below the dais. The President consulted his watch with satisfaction.

'A special meeting will be called in exactly two hours time, Colonel Darcy,' he said. 'Subject: The selection of a new Cabinet.'

The Colonel saluted. 'Yes, My President,' he said in tones of deep respect. He saluted and went out, his heavy boots clittering over the marble floor; he ushered out the last of the white-coated attendants and the door closed behind them. The President seemed to become fully aware of General Smithers for the first time.

'You wished to see me, General?'

President Trygon smiled benignly but the gesture died stillborn on his face, killed by his wide slit of a mouth and the combination of the silver eye-patch and the gold monocle. The silver triangle over his left eye winked like the glare of a sunspot every time it caught the light.

Smithers stiffened and marched forward towards the foot of Trygon's dais.

'Yes, My President. The matter I mentioned earlier. Espionage, violation of air space and overt acts against the State.'

Trygon nodded. 'Ah, yes. A serious affair. The prisoner Faraday is here?'

Smithers nodded ponderously. 'Yes, My President. Colonel Roderick Usher is in charge of the case.'

Smithers marched to the side of the dais and stood at attention.

'Prisoner and escort forward. Colonel Usher, will you please read the charges.'

Trygon sat and smoked as Usher got some papers out of a brief-case he took off a table in the alcove. I was marched across in front of Trygon, at the top of the U-shaped table, with the two officers behind me.

One of them whispered to me laconically, 'Prisoners don't address the President, neither do they interrupt. One word from you and I'll blow your head off.'

I made a mental note to take him off my social list. I stood and studied the madman in the green and gold uniform as Usher read out the charges from his documents. They were very formal, with a liberal sprinkling of whereases and enemies of the state. The principal charges were as Smithers had said. Hostile acts against Trygon's kingdom; espionage, industrial and military; violation of air space; the taking of aerial photographs, apparently a capital offence. This pantomime went on for about ten minutes. Usher finally stopped reading and put the documents back in his brief-case.

'These facts are fully attested?' snapped Trygon. He hadn't even looked at me.

'Yes, My President,' said Smithers servilely.

'Very well,' said Trygon, his silver eye-patch catching the light as he moved his great domed head. 'The protocol is quite clear. Capital offences, standard punishments laid down. A civilian, so no military honours. You have the papers there?'

Smithers clicked to attention and advanced to Trygon's dais. He handed up a document which bore an impressive seal. Trygon took it languidly between podgy fingers. He barely glanced at it as he laid it on the desk extension before him. His pen made a high scratching sound in the silence as he scribbled something on it.

'Given under my seal,' he said crisply. 'Sentence of death. No confirmation necessary. Execution to take place immediately by firing squad. You may retire.'

From first to last he hadn't so much as flicked an eyelid in my direction. I think I resented him even more for that.

'Thank you, My President,' said Smithers. He saluted again and retired. 'You may proceed, Colonel Usher.'

Usher turned to me, his jaw twitching.

'Prisoner and escort, forward march!'

Chapter Fifteen

Delayed Execution

1

The sound of eight feet slapping the marble floor of Trygon's Conference Chamber was like the ticking of a clock in a condemned man's cell. Trygon had already turned away and we were wheeling back from the U-shaped table when Usher broke protocol with a tremendous gesture.

'Escort, halt!' His voice sounded like a whip-crack and was followed a second later by, 'Permission to speak, My President!'

I caught a glimpse of Smithers standing like a man turned to stone, his stout body apparently sculpted in a servile bow, one foot behind him before retiring from the throne. Trygon's pink dome looked like a Turner sunset. His gold monocle didn't exactly drop out of his remaining eye but it looked as though it might; I could have sworn his eye-muscles relaxed to a miniscule extent and then iron discipline re-asserted itself and his jaw tautened.

He spoke in a terrible voice, his bloodshot eye blank behind the gold rim. The silver patch looked like a baleful fire that might at any moment overflow its confines and lap the whole room.

'You have, I hope, a good reason Colonel Usher, for this unprecedented breach of discipline?'

Usher had recovered himself. His face was impassive as he replied, 'Certainly, My President.'

Trygon crossed his legs, lolled back in his leather padded armchair and said arrogantly, 'You may advance to explain your reasons.'

Usher marched up to the foot of the dais. I stayed where I was, pinioned by the two officers. One of them had put his pistol back in his holster but the other had his jammed in the broad of my back.

'I have no brief for the late Leopold Zilar or his colleagues,' said Usher in a level voice. 'But there was a grain of sense in one of two of the things which he said.'

Trygon stirred on his seat; the innocuous movement sent an almost tangible breath of danger out from his menacing figure. I could see Usher waver in his determination, such was the power radiated by Trygon's squat form.

'Be brief, Colonel Usher,' he said softly.

'My submission is this, sir,' Usher went on. 'There have been violations of air space, certain incidents on the border. The American authorities may well be alerted. This might be dangerous at a time when we are undertaking delicate negotiations. Would it not be prudent to find out exactly what this spy knows? Or in other words what the outside world knows? In order that we may take measures against them.'

Trygon appeared to turn this over in his mind for a moment. He crossed his legs the other way. I noticed he was wearing dark tan riding boots with what appeared to be gold ornamental spurs.

'Your remarks have some application, Colonel Usher. What is your suggestion?'

'Let me have this man for a few hours,' said Usher. 'There are ways of extracting the information from him. He is to die anyway. My suggestion is that his execution be postponed until dawn.'

Trygon glanced at the clock on the console before him; he had already made up his mind before he turned back to Usher.

'Request granted,' he said. 'Three hours. Make a note, General Smithers.'

2

We were in a room with a concrete floor, metal walls and a steel ceiling that reflected back the light in blinding sheets. I'd passed out once but the shorter of the two junior officers had just poured the second bucket of water over me. I lay on the floor and listened to the top of my head flying through the air and then slamming back again. I put up my hand and felt crusted blood on the side of my forehead.

'You're getting nowhere, Colonel Usher,' said the Captain, whose name was Kreschmann, for the fourth or fifth time. 'We've wasted an hour already.'

The second of the officers was guarding the door outside.

'He's tough all right,' said Usher, taking the leather glove off his right hand. 'But I'll break him down.'

'The President expects results,' Kreschmann warned him. 'We'd better come through on this.'

'You worry too much,' Usher said. 'Have you ever known me fall down on the job?'

Kreschmann tightened his lips but didn't answer him. I looked at Usher through half-closed eyes. I didn't think he was the sort of pistol who would fall down on the job. He swung his arm at my face almost casually. Now I was strapped down to a metal framework that racked out from the wall so I couldn't dodge. Lights exploded in brilliant patterns as he patted my jaw. My head slapped to one side and Usher went on cuffing me. I tasted blood again and the side of my jaw began a dull throbbing. My face seemed completely detached from the rest of my body.

He went on giving me lefts and rights which made high cracking noises which re-echoed back from the ceiling. I saw red-pointed stars and while I was counting the points of light I must have passed out again. I came around while they were unstrapping me. I had a job to stand and Kreschmann had to support me.

Usher picked up the side of the room and hit me with it. Kreschmann lifted a boot the size of a house. It came forward in slow motion, the black leather shining dully under the glow of the lamps. I was on a rocket to the moon, arced out beyond the farthest stars. I began to fall back towards the earth like a spent firework. While I was on the ground someone drove a herd of cattle over me. When I was spread around over half an acre someone else came out and worked over what was left with a coke-hammer.

Usher was tired and Kreschmann must have taken over next time I was conscious. I was choking to death; water ran down my face and shoulders. I heard Usher say, 'That's no good. You'll kill him and we'll never get the information.'

I had an idea then and managed to move my head. A rasping croak sounded in the silence of the room. I was shocked to hear it was my own voice. Kreschmann put down the steel-tipped riding switch he was using. The room swam back into my vision. Kreschmann was stripped to the waist and moisture ran down the thick hair which matted his chest and shone like oil on the bunched muscles of his shoulders. Usher's face was impassive; only his scar shone whitely on his cheek. He glanced up at the metal-cased clock on the wall. 'It's been two hours. Looks like you were right.'

Kreschmann lifted the whip again.

'Wait,' I said. The word came out of my throat in a bubbling rush. Kreschmann waited, the steel tip of the whip poised over his shoulder, little flecks of light shining on it.

'I'll tell you what you want to know,' I said. 'Take me to your President.'

It was a bit of dialogue I'd always wanted to say and now I had the opportunity. Kreschmann laughed and flung down the whip in triumph. Usher relaxed and his face broke open in a smile.

'Good boy,' he said. 'Now you got some sense.'

Kreschmann wiped his chest with a towel and started putting on his shirt and tunic. Usher untied me. I was surprised to find I was strung up from two metal rings set in a beam in the ceiling. I must have been out longer than I thought. I put my head down near my knees and twisted my muscles, relaxing the ache in my wrists and shoulders.

'We'd better get him cleaned up first,' Usher told Kreschmann.

The two of them half dragged me into a small washroom in the corridor adjoining. Kreschmann stayed in the doorway while Usher put a soapy flannel over my face. The hot water stung but it brought the life back to me. I took the flannel from him and sponged gingerly at my forehead and face. My cheekbones were bruised and cut about but I wasn't roughed up so much as I had thought.

By the time I'd finished patching myself up and had knotted my tie I looked quite presentable in half light and providing anyone didn't look too closely. With Usher by my side and the two junior officers behind me we walked back down the corridor for my second interview with President Trygon.

3

Trygon's single eye was like an angry sunset within the frame of the gold monocle. He sat in his padded chair and smoked a Turkish cigarette through a long holder as Usher made a preliminary report. The silver eye-patch burned bright flame as his pink-domed head moved impatiently beneath the lamps. He glanced at my battered face as I stood between Kreschmann and the other officer. 'A very sensible attitude, Mr . . . ,' he said benevolently, searching for my surname.

'Faraday.' It was Usher who had supplied it for him.

It was the first time Trygon had looked at me with conscious volition and I felt his single eye take in all the details he felt to be relevant to his purposes.

'What do you believe in, Mr Faraday?' he asked softly.

169

'Personal stoicism,' I said. 'In this world you just grit your teeth and go on.'

Trygon glanced round the vast Conference Chamber with approval. His gaze rested on Usher and then passed back to me. He laughed. It was a startling sound. His pink dome turned a deep russet colour.

'Excellent, Mr Faraday. A highly personal philosophy and a proper one for a soldier. I like that.'

He snapped his teeth together as though he were chewing off the end of his sentence and waited for me to continue.

Usher broke the silence for the second time.

'Spill it,' he said impatiently. 'The President wants to know why you came here and what you learned.'

I told them. I made like I was more beat up than I was. It seemed to impress Trygon at any rate. I didn't know about Usher. General Smithers came in halfway through my recital; he listened impassively but his eyes expressed satisfaction at my battered condition.

'Too many lorries had been disappearing,' I said. 'The truck operators didn't like it.'

Trygon gave a thin smile; it was like the rictus on the face of a dead lizard.

'We could not permit violation of our borders,' the President said. 'These men were trespassers. They were dealt with and their lorries impounded.'

'How did you think you could get away with

170

it?' I asked. Not really expecting an answer. But Trygon gave me one anyway. He cleared his throat with a rasping cough.

'Four men,' he said. 'Four men against a state. Do you think anyone is going to bother about the fate of a few truck drivers compared with the important affairs we have on hand?'

'Someone did,' I said. 'They called me in.'

Trygon looked at me sharply. 'You are already a condemned man,' he said with infinite contempt. 'Hardly convincing proof of your theory.'

'Not just me,' I said. 'You forget about the aircraft. We took photographs. And what about the business at the Park-Plaza?'

There was a long silence. Trygon froze the movement of his head and sat as though turned to bronze. Smithers was the first to shake the spell. Hysteria was blurring the edges of his voice.

'Do you not think things are getting out of hand, My President?' he asked. 'We have already lost Dillon. The American police will have investigated his background.'

He fell silent, struck mute by the imperious wave of the President's hand.

'Ah, yes, Dillon,' said the President. 'I had overlooked that. One of our best. Leader of No 1 Liquidation Unit. For that alone you would merit the death penalty, Mr Faraday.'

'And Krish, My President,' Kreschmann reminded Trygon. 'Because of the man

171

Faraday we had to dispose of Krish as well.'

Kreschmann seemed to be forgetting protocol under the stress of the moment. I figured Krish would have been the man with the bow tie and jug ears who had been dumped in my car. It seemed like centuries ago. And in another country.

'Krish was a fool,' said Trygon cuttingly. 'As Chief of Security and officer in charge of all customs posts he was a complete failure. And as to Dillon, his elimination has meant promotion for an even more valuable officer. Eh, Colonel Usher?'

Usher stiffened to the salute. 'As you say, sir,' he said sardonically.

Trygon chuckled and shifted on his padded chair. The tense atmosphere in the Conference Chamber started to dissipate.

'Mr Faraday's information, valuable as it may be to him, hardly affects the great issues facing this country. Or the even more important decisions being made shortly. What does it all amount to? A few inquiries by a private detective; a small aircraft takes some pictures; a few truck drivers disappear. By the time all these events have been painfully pieced together by the civil authorities our work here will be finished. No, I do not think we need worry. The man Faraday has had his painful experience for nothing. He could have told us what little he knew in the beginning and could have been shot and buried by now.'

172

'Thanks very much,' I said mildly.

I thought I saw Usher's jaw muscles relax ever so slightly in a miniscule smile. Smithers' jaw hung slackly as my impertinence penetrated his consciousness.

'That will be all then, gentlemen,' Trygon said. 'Everything is under control. Sentence to stand. Colonel Usher to see that it is carried out.'

'One more favour, sir,' said Usher, standing stiffly to attention again. 'I'd like to do this myself. Personally.'

He slapped the pistol butt at his belt. 'Dillon was quite a friend of mine.'

The gold monocle came round and fixed Usher in an unwinking stare.

'Sentimental nonsense, of course, Colonel Usher, but entirely understandable. Permission granted.'

'Thank you, My President.'

Usher's boot heels clicked together in an immaculate explosion of sound on the marble floor. The four of us wheeled back towards the big doors again. Smithers stayed behind with the President.

Kreschmann and the other junior officer kept behind us. Usher got out his revolver and checked it. We whined downwards in another elevator. The second officer disappeared through the doorway of a brightly lit hut as we got outside in the open air. The wind blew cold but it was a fine starry night. We went along a concrete ramp in front of storage bays and factory buildings. Red-painted machinery reared skywards. It looked like some sort of ore-crushing plant. There seemed to be acres of it.

We went down a ramp and in a metal door and along another concrete corridor lit with dim lamps. Usher unlocked a large wooden door and gestured me in with his pistol. I was in a small room about ten feet square. I heard a whispered conversation behind me and then Usher came in alone. The barrel of his pistol seemed to grow until it filled all the room.

'Up against the wall, Mr Faraday,' he said in a voice of infinite regret. 'And put your hands above your head.'

I did as he said. The concrete felt cold and damp against my fingers. All the nerves and muscles in my shoulders and back were tense and I could feel the small hairs on the back of my neck erect like a cat. I looked round desperately for something which would give me a chance but I didn't come up with anything.

The revolver cracked with a slam that seemed like the end of the world. Bright lights, choking smoke and nothingness as I slid to the ground into the darkness of death.

Chapter Sixteen

Dawn Rises Again

1

I was still alive. I lay on the concrete and watched a beetle scurry off into the rim of darkness at the edge of the room. The side of my head ached and cordite fumes were choking me. Chunks of concrete littered the floor. As consciousness returned I saw the big hole Usher's bullet had made in the wall. That was where the chips of concrete had come from. One of them had caught me on the side of the head causing me to pass out temporarily.

I felt Usher's hand on my neck, pressing me down on to the floor. I stiffened, waiting for the coup de grace. Unbelievable that he could have missed at that range. Usher turned me over to face him. His eyes were dancing with strange lights.

'Gaton. F.B.I.,' he said crisply. 'Sorry about that but I had to make it look for real. Haven't time to explain. Act dead.'

I didn't need asking twice. I closed my eyes and sprawled out, my limbs relaxed. I heard the door open and then the scrape of boots on the floor. Kreschmann came over into the middle of the room. He kicked me twice in the ribs. I forced my muscles to go limp. I figured I would settle with him later. With interest. He laughed. I heard the low rumble of conversation.

'Tell the President,' Usher said. 'That's an order.'

Kreschmann's boots clicked on the concrete. 'Yes, Colonel!' he said. He went out and slammed the door behind him.

Usher knelt down by me. 'Take it easy,' he whispered. 'We've got perhaps fifteen minutes. You'd better have this.'

I opened my eyes as he slid the Smith-Wesson across the floor to me. It felt like an old friend as I got my hand round the butt.

Usher put his arm round my shoulder and helped me up and into a chair. I choked as he put the rim of a metal flask into my mouth. Raw spirit dribbled out of my lips but some went down my throat. The warmth of the brandy spread throughout my body. I held my hand over my mouth to suppress a fit of coughing. Steps sounded in the corridor. Usher went over towards the door, making a warning gesture with his hand. The footsteps passed by. He locked the door from the inside and came back.

'We haven't got long,' he said. 'So I'll make it brief.'

I got up unsteadily.

'Before I forget it—thanks,' I said.

176

Usher's scar stood out whitely as he smiled. 'You've been in my way since you came on the scene,' he said. 'I've had one hell of a time thinking up methods of preventing Trygon's boys from picking you off.'

He got out a pack of cigarettes, put two in his mouth, lit them and handed me one. I blew out the smoke gratefully. Usher sat down with his pistol in his hand and kept an eye on the door.

'Trygon's crazy, of course. He got thrown out of South America just after the war. This set-up is a dream of his from way back. It took the Bureau over five years to get this far. It's taken me personally over two years to get on the inside. So I couldn't have you balling it up.'

'What's the racket?' I asked.

Usher shrugged. 'Just one of the richest uranium deposits you ever laid eyes on. Trygon cornered the real estate in this part of the world before the war. A mining engineer first stumbled on it. Trygon was employing him at the time. On this character's advice Trygon started buying up tracts of land. It was all desolate canyon so no-one had any objections. The mining engineer got killed later. An accident, the coroner said.'

Usher gave me a cynical smile. 'Private empires and the cornering of the uranium market just aren't on in the atomic age,' he went on. 'So the F.B.I. started following up a few trails. Trygon's got it in for this country.

He got an eye knocked out in a tussle with the U.S. coastguards during a spot of Cuban blockade running. The setting up of a state within a state with himself as the President became an obsession with him. As his operations spread he found himself a multi-millionaire. The Bureau, working with the C.I.A. boys, knew there were more supplies of uranium finding their way on to the world market than was justified through the existing sources. There had to be another source that no-one knew about. Trygon was the supply.'

I looked around the small concrete room. 'How come anyone could operate a private empire in California without the authorities knowing?'

Usher turned to face me. His eyes looked an even brighter blue beneath the lamps.

'It started off as a building operation,' he said. 'There was no difficulty about that part, nor for the tile factory that followed. And anyone can buy up war surplus, even tanks.'

I waited for him to go on.

'The recruiting of his army was the difficult part. And he wanted technicians too. But money can buy anything. Most of his strong-arm boys are professional soldiers, hired mercenaries, Cuban adventurers and the like. Anyone disaffected or with a grudge against Uncle Sam. The salaries are astronomical and they live like princes here. They serve an agreed term and when their time's up they're shipped out of the States.'

'Or dropped overboard?' I asked.

Usher shrugged again. 'Your guess is as good as mine. But it seems on the cards to me.'

'How did you get in?' I said.

'Too long to go into now,' said Usher. 'More than two years, like I said. Trygon's got a big deal coming off in the morning. A deal that's got to be stopped. I only heard about it last night. Too late to let my F.B.I. contact know. Trygon's fixing to supply uranium on a large scale to Red China.'

'Which is where Mr Pen Ching comes in,' I said.

Usher stubbed out his cigarette against a corner of the table. 'I got to hand it to you, Faraday,' he said. 'You don't miss a trick. The Bureau could do with a few like you.'

'We're not asleep in L.A.,' I said.

Usher smiled again. 'That leaves us just a few hours before he fixes everything up with the Chinese delegates.'

'Why the helicopter when they could simply have driven up the road?' I asked.

'Trygon's power mad,' said Usher. 'This is the approach laid on to impress all visitors who add up to anything.'

'Do you mind filling in a few pieces?' I said.

'Like what?' he said.

'The house in the canyon. April Dawn. The man with the jug ears who was dumped in my car. To be going on with.'

Usher went over to the door and listened. Almost ten minutes had gone by while we'd been talking. He came back again. He gave the revolver to me.

'A spare,' he said with a grim smile. 'I'll go get my machine pistol before we break out of here.'

'The canyon set-up,' I persisted.

'Shangri-La was used as a sort of advance warning post,' Usher said.

I blinked at him.

'The house with the Chinese gateway,' Usher went on stubbornly.

'April Dawn and the fake professor were supposed to handle that end. Hilton's here. He acts as a sort of public relations man with a smattering of scientific knowledge. He was quite a useful front together with the girl. I don't care about him but I want Smithers alive. He knows the whole shebang.'

'It's Kreschmann I'm after,' I said. There must have been something in my voice. Usher's face changed.

'I'm sorry about the roughing up,' he said. 'But I had to make it look real. I held him up as long as possible and then Kreschmann insisted on taking over.'

'Don't mention it,' I said. 'But Kreschmann's mine.'

'Fine,' Usher said.

'You must have passed a few tough moments if you were on the murder squad,'

I said.

Usher didn't reply for a moment. When he did his voice had gone hard again.

'I can say I didn't have to kill anyone,' he said. 'At least not until tonight. And I managed to save a few people too.'

'Like who?' I said.

Usher grinned suddenly. Even his scar looked benevolent.

'Like you,' he said. 'Up Tintoretto Canyon the other day. I fired wide to warn you. Remember? After the helicopter went over. Otherwise Dillon would have done the job for real.'

I stared at him, groping for words. When I could get them out I said, 'Then it was you on the Park-Plaza roof as well? The tall man in the sweater who frightened Bishop to death when he came down the ladder?'

Usher nodded slowly. 'The fat man, yes. You did me a good turn when you got Dillon. I managed to jog his elbow when he fired at you with the compressed-air pistol. He had his suspicions of me then but you kept him too busy. If you hadn't fixed him I'd have been next on his list. So it looks like we're all square.'

He put out his second cigarette and pitched the butt on to the floor. I glanced at my watch. The fifteen minutes mentioned by Usher or Gatin—I couldn't remember which to call him now—were almost up.

'What happened to Krish?' he said.

I had to think hard before I recollected who he meant. The throbbing in my head seemed to be getting worse.

'The gentleman with the jug-ears? I dumped him down the canyon.'

Usher bared his teeth in a noiseless laugh. 'And Dillon and I had quite a time getting him into your Buick. Krish was getting careless. He left the last truckie's body out for someone to find. So he had to go. I like your style, Faraday, as I said before. I'd have given something to have seen your face.'

'So would I,' I said 'Fortunately it was dark at the time.'

Usher glanced down at his own watch. He went over to the door and listened for a moment. I remembered something else while he was doing that.

'Why Roderick Usher?' I asked.

He shot me a quick smile. 'Edgar Allan Poe is one of my favourite authors.'

He unlocked the door, making no attempt at quietness. He motioned me to get behind it. I heard him go down the corridor and call someone. There were hurried footsteps. A long silence followed. Then I heard a bump and a groan. There was a scraping noise and Usher re-entered the room, crouching. He was dragging with him the second of the two junior officers; he was deeply unconscious and breathing through the nose.

The two of us began to strip him. Then Usher went back into the corridor. He returned and locked the door behind him.

'I forgot his cap,' he said simply.

He jammed it on my head. We gagged the officer with two handkerchiefs; one stuffed into a ball in his mouth, the other to hold it in, and then trussed him with some rope Usher produced from a cupboard in the corner. Fortunately the officer was about my fit. While I was changing my clothes Usher checked the unconscious man's Browning.

'What's your F.B.I. link?' I asked him.

He shook his head. 'We shan't be able to do anything in time. I don't break cover and my contact isn't due to get in touch for several days.'

'My secretary has instructions to call the L.A. police,' I said, 'but the timing isn't right either.'

'We'll just have to go it alone,' Usher said.

He regarded the bound form of the heavily breathing officer; he was an incongruous sight in black and white striped underpants and a pink singlet.

'Still,' he mused, 'that only leaves about 199 members of the garrison for us to deal with. Reasonable odds.'

I fished in the pocket of the uniform jacket and found some dark cheaters. I put these on. I opened the webbing holster at my belt and put the pistol Usher had given me in there. I held my Smith-Wesson at my side. We left the room without concealment, Usher locking the door after us. We marched straight down the corridor, our feet making clicks which echoed back from the metal walls. I waited for a long moment while Usher went into his own room. He came back with his machine pistol. He handed me my documents and other personal belongings. I stuffed them in my pockets.

We passed into the open air and across a concrete yard where hooded trucks were parked. Beyond red danger notices lamps on tall standards burned. Near the hangar area was a compound. Usher unlocked it with a key on a bunch he carried in his hand. We went through two more wire fences. Eventually, Usher unlocked three different padlocks on a thick metal-faced door. A brilliant bar of light came from inside as he opened it and beckoned me through. We went down the broad aisle between complex masses of machinery.

He opened another door with a double lock. We stepped inside and then a fury of blonde hair and whirling fists rushed through the air. Small hands pummelled at my chest. I fell sideways against the wall while something sharp drew blood from my cheeks.

Usher laughed loudly in the silence of the room.

'Meet April Dawn,' he said.

Chapter Seventeen

Ordeal by Water

1

I blinked. 'Take it easy,' I said. Usher pinioned the girl's hands behind her. He went over and whispered into her ear. Her expression changed. All the fire and hatred went out of her eyes. She looked quickly from Usher back to me.

'Is this true?'

Usher nodded. 'We've come to help you,' he said in a low voice. 'Just keep it up and leave us to do the rest.'

Even in her present dishevelled state the girl really looked something. She wore faded blue jeans and a black and white tailored check shirt. There was something about her that made the fake April Dawn look like a paste imitation compared with the real thing in the window of Tiffany's. My mind was doing quick flips readjusting to Usher's shock statement.

By the time we had gone across the big room, skirting more banks of machinery, my brain had sifted the information and appraised it. Guess my head wasn't working properly after Kreschmann's going-over. Our footsteps clattered on the floor as we came around the last bank, the girl between us. Underneath the brilliant light thrown downwards by a multi-socket lighting fixture, a grey-haired man of about sixty-five was spread-eagled. His wrists and ankles were secured by metal clips which stretched him like an insect on a mounting blotter. His hair and beard glinted silver under the lamps and tears of pain ran out of the corners of his eyes. His extremities were blue.

His body and the lower parts of his arms and legs were immersed in a shallow tank, just deep enough to cover his entire body. Chrome taps winked in the bright light and steam rose from the surface of the water as a figure bending over him directed a jet of boiling water into the ice-cold flood which already surrounded the old man. He stiffened and a bubbling scream came out of his mouth.

The squat figure in the peaked cap with a rat-trap for a mouth and two holes bored in his face for eyes increased the flow. 'Co-operate and you get better treatment,' he said. 'Otherwise you go back in the Hole.'

The old man whimpered but his spirit hadn't been broken. He tried to spit at the soldier who wore master-sergeant's stripes and smiled down at him placidly but the saliva merely dribbled down his own cheek. There was a crack as the heavy butt of a leather-plaited whip in the sergeant's hands came up and a red weal appeared on the victim's face.

He sagged back and appeared to be unconscious. The girl had broken from us with a cry and was trying to raise the old man's head.

'How's it going, Kowalski?' said Usher pleasantly. 'This is Captain Travis.'

The sergeant nodded at me distantly and scowled at Usher. 'I'd say we're wasting time here, Colonel. Wash him down the drain and get a physics man who's prepared to co-operate. That's my philosophy.'

Usher nodded like he was impressed by the argument and walked over to where the girl April Dawn was wiping the old man's forehead with her handkerchief. I walked around the table, moving softly on the balls of my feet, holding the Smith-Wesson hidden against the folds of my uniform tunic. I hit Kowalski with all the strength I'd got on the side of the face. The barrel of the Smith-Wesson made a cracking sound and Kowalski went out in mid-sentence. His eyes closed, his face turned grey and he went crashing down against the edge of the table. He left a red smear on the edge of it. I wiped the barrel of my revolver on his shirt. Usher was already relieving him of his own pistol. He bent down and felt Kowalski's heart.

'I think you killed him,' he said mildly. He looked up at me and smiled encouragingly. 'Not that I think anyone will mind.'

The girl was already releasing the old man as we dragged Kowalski over to a cupboard and locked him in.

'It was rather an informal introduction just now,' Usher said. 'The real April Dawn and the real Professor Hilton were unfortunate enough to rent Shangri-La a few months ago. Their presence at the gateway of Trygon's kingdom called for drastic measures. With the house empty there was no risk of discovery but Trygon couldn't have strangers in his own backyard. He kidnapped the pair and substituted his own facsimiles, the late Marlene Travers, a small-time actress and Karl Koch, who played Hilton. Trygon had first found out that the girl and her uncle had only just come out to the West Coast so no-one knew them in the area. Trygon's got a crush on April Dawn and has been forcing her to write letters to relatives from the Canyon house to let them know all's well.'

'Why the torture act?' I asked, helping the girl and Usher to lift Professor Hilton out of the metal bath. His thin body, clad only in bathing trunks, was pinched and blue and his breathing jerky and erratic.

'You'll find some blankets over there,' Usher told the girl. 'He happens to be a real professor of physics who'd be useful to Trygon in the uranium caper,' said Usher to me. 'He also happens to be an honest man who likes this country.'

We carried the professor over into a corner, wrapped him in the thick grey blankets the girl had produced and Usher forced the flask into his mouth. His eyelids flickered once or twice but otherwise there was no visible sign that the spirit was having any effect.

'This here's Mike Faraday, a private eye from L.A. who's come to get us out of this mess,' said Usher sardonically to the girl. 'No time to explain now. Look after the old man and take your cues from us.'

The girl stared up at us like a small child trying to stop from crying. She meant to smile but her lower lip trembled. Usher walked me back to the torture tank whose shining taps stuck up at odd angles like a film producer's idea of Martian gadgetry.

'There's just one thing I ought to make clear, Faraday,' Usher said. 'It's a fine point of protocol but it's got to be observed, just in case anything happens to me.'

'What could happen to you?' I said. 'You're immortal. You said so yourself. Anyone who's had two years of this has got to be death-proof.'

'Nevertheless, when things start popping, don't go berserk,' Usher said. 'Trygon, Kreschmann, Koch, anyone else, yes; they're fair targets. But the Red China delegates are different. Especially Mr Pen Ching who's a big wheel over there. Although we don't recognize Mao's crowd, we can't afford a showdown on an international scale. And this would blow up into a dangerous incident straight away.'

'What's the drill, then?' I said.

'Protocol,' said Usher, with a lazy smile. 'No violence so far as the red peril is concerned. We just declare them persona non grata and quietly extradite them. And I don't think they'll give us any trouble either.'

'I hope I can distinguish a Chinese from a Cuban in the smoke,' I said.

'That's my department,' Usher replied.

I looked round the room again before we went out.

'Wait till Ronald Reagan hears about this,' I said.

2

We left April Dawn and her uncle in the corner, locking the door behind us. The girl seemed more normal and her uncle was coming round. Usher told her to stay put until we came back. We went through the concrete yard and out the compound, Usher unlocking and re-locking the gates behind us. The faint streaks of dawn were beginning to paint the sky in the east. We crept past the open door of a guardroom; blue cigarette smoke escaped into the night and loud laughter came across the yard to us.

'I'm making for the truck park,' Usher whispered to me. 'Unless we can knock out the heavy stuff we shan't make much impression.'

Usher had the machine pistol and I had the

Smith-Wesson at the ready with the officer's pistol in my left hand as a spare. We soon found the park; there were about a dozen big trucks and no less than four tanks, Trygon's main striking force. There were no guards.

'The rest of the stuff's scattered all over the canyon,' Usher said. 'Jeeps, light machine gun trucks and so on. I don't think they'll have time to get to them if we can knock this out. Trouble is, I want one tank in reserve. They're pretty close for what I have in mind.'

He disappeared into the shadows. I sat down against the wheel of one of the big trucks and kept my eyes peeled. Presently Usher came back. He had a metal cylinder on his back and tubing glinted in the faint light from the sky. He started buckling the outfit on.

'Get some cans of gas and slop it around,' he whispered. 'I want to make this good. I shall be pretty vulnerable if there's any lead flying around.'

He adjusted the nozzle of the flame-thrower and started putting a heavy mask over his face as I went down the park. I found a dump of gasoline, the heavy cans secured under a tarpaulin. It took me twenty minutes to slop the gas around. I covered all the lorries and three of the tanks. Usher was very particular about this. He'd already had a look at the fourth, a heavily-armoured job which stood by itself, away from the other three. I was just dumping the last of my cans and Usher had gone back into the shadow of one of the tanks when a voice broke the silence.

'Drop the gun, Faraday, or you're a dead man.'

The character I'd known as Professor Hilton but who was really Karl Koch came forward into the faint light. Behind him was the burly form of Kreschmann. Koch carried a machine pistol cradled in the crook of his arm. Kreschmann had a sub-machine gun. The stench of gasoline hung heavily on the air as they stepped out of cover towards me.

Chapter Eighteen

Tank Warfare

1

'You'd better slow up,' I said. 'One pop from that thing and we'll all be frying.'

Kreschmann stopped as though a fist had struck him.

'Hold it, Koch,' he said sharply. He sniffed the air like a dog. He bared his teeth at me in a grimace.

'What would you suggest?'

'An armed truce,' I said. I put down the can I'd been using and straightened up. The three of us stood in a triangle. Behind the truck about five yards away and slightly in rear of Kreschmann and Koch was Usher. He had the nozzle of the flame-thrower pointed in our direction and I could almost hear his thoughts. The shrouded forms of the trucks and the heavy tanks were slowly being etched in by the strengthening dawn light.

Koch's hand trembled on the trigger of the machine pistol. I could see he might risk a shot, taking me chest high, hoping that the gasoline wouldn't explode; I waited until I saw his fingers change the setting over to single-shot. I could see that Kreschmann with his experience, wouldn't shoot at that stage. I jumped low as the shot cracked out, landed a yard away and went rolling towards the open area. Usher opened up then with his flame-thrower, retreating as he sprayed. I couldn't see what Kreschmann was doing.

The crump of the explosion as the gasoline went up blew me along the ground with surprising gentleness; I saw the sky and the earth change places and then flame bloomed and filled the whole of the universe. Above the roaring crackle I could hear Koch scream; he staggered a few yards like a fireball, his hands still welded to the machine pistol. His hair blazed like a torch and the whole of his body suddenly seemed to fall to pieces, flaking to the ground; charred bone, surrounded by a halo of crimson.

The trucks were all crackling brightly as I

came to a stop; I still had the Smith-Wesson in my hand. I could see Usher silhouetted against the flames. He kept spraying at the shrouded masses of the tanks. I could hear shouts and running footsteps from far off. I looked round for Kreschmann. He was lying about ten feet away from me; his uniform cap had fallen off and the sub-machine gun was lying about a yard from his outstretched hand.

I got up as he rolled over, lifting the Thompson; I jumped on the run, both my feet landing with a heavy crack on his wrist. The gun went down and stayed there. Kreschmann got up, clawing at the pistol at his belt. His eyes were narrow slits of hate and fear. The pistol blasted skywards as I got my left hand to his wrist. I tried to bring the Smith-Wesson up but he jacked his knee into my stomach; I went down, gasping for breath.

When my vision cleared I could see Kreschmann several yards away, silhouetted against the flames. Behind him was Usher, who had just unbuckled the flame-thrower. Kreschmann brought the barrel of the pistol up as I put three shots into his back. The muzzle of the Smith-Wesson jumped a little as I stitched him across. Kreschmann stiffened and seemed to hang suspended against the backdrop of blazing trucks. Small flames lapped at his uniform jacket; the barrel of the Thompson hit the ground and he collapsed like a doll.

I went over to Kreschmann and turned him over; black blood ran out of his mouth and nose and his eyes were wide open. I heard the heavy rumble of a tank then. There were a long series of explosions and I could see the three tanks ablaze; the fourth was rumbling out of the darkness at me. It stopped, with a throbbing of motors; I could see Usher's head in the turret as shots sounded somewhere behind me.

'For Christ's sake,' said Usher irritably. 'Jump aboard. We haven't got all night!'

2

I clambered down into the turret and Usher shut the hatch after us. I re-loaded the Smith-Wesson while he was doing this and put it back in my holster.

'You know how to work one of these?' said Usher.

'You're joking,' I told him.

He grinned in the dim blue glow of the fighting lights inside the tank. There was a heavy smell of grease, diesel oil and cordite in here.

'Never mind,' he said. 'You can take over when we've picked April Dawn up.'

He sat down in the bucket seat and looked out through the slit to one side; in the big, bulletproof mirror I could see the parking bay ahead and small running figures on the concrete. Usher moved a lever and the monster came to life; the earth shuddered, the big diesels revved up and then we were lumbering over the ground at what seemed an astonishing speed. Usher pulled another lever and we started to turn. Then we skirted the blazing lorry park, which was still exploding skywards and crashed our way through the compound. The wire and concrete post fence went down like sticks of celery before the Sherman.

'Trygon's modified all this stuff for his own use,' said Usher, as we jolted across the compound. 'I think it was to provide something for the technicians to do rather than for any practical purpose. A Sherman chassis and armour; light machine guns which are non-standard; and a six-pounder he got from Swiss sources. Makes a pretty formidable outfit, though.'

I glanced around the interior which seemed surprisingly roomy; there was another lurch as we went through the second compound fence. I could see electric lamp standards coming up and then Usher put the Sherman straight at the side of the wall before us. There was a noise like the Waldorf-Astoria had fallen on top of us, the fighting lights flickered and choking dust drifted in through the battle slits. Usher's blue eyes were alight with pleasure and excitement.

'What price Bastogne now!' he said. 'It isn't

every day I get carte blanche to wreck property on this scale.'

The motors throbbed on as he got up to the turret; it took the two of us to lift the lid. When we had cleared the splintered timber I found we were just inside the entrance of the machine room where we'd been earlier that night. A pair of jack-booted legs were trying to crawl away from under the debris. Usher pounced and caught hold of them. I put the barrel of the Smith-Wesson against the back of the man's head. He turned terror-stricken eyes to us, in which the eyeballs were merely yellow slits.

'Don't shoot,' he moaned. 'I don't want to die.'

'How did he ever get to be a General?' I asked Usher, looking at Smithers' greasy face.

'Influence and the right relatives,' Usher said. He leaned down and plucked Smithers' revolver out of his holster; he hurled it far into the night.

'Watch him,' he said to me.

He went off down the machine room, jingling his keys. I stood against the tank tracks and listened to the heavy throbbing of the motors. I kept my gun ready by my side and watched Smithers' sweating face. He swallowed heavily several times, as he looked imploringly at me. He had his chin where his navel should have been. I was afraid he would bust out crying but Usher saved me from that.

I saw him coming back with April Dawn; they were supporting the Professor between them. The old boy was conscious; he was fully dressed in an oversize uniform I figured had been taken from Kowalski but apart from his tailoring he didn't look too bad. We waited while Usher and the girl got the old man up in the turret and down inside the tank. I could hear a few scattered shots over near the blazing trucks; someone was obviously attempting to organize a counter-attack and some trigger-happy characters were shooting at shadows.

I got Smithers up into the turret and then shut the hatch behind me; there didn't seem to be much room in here now with five of us. I gave April Dawn my spare pistol and told her to watch Smithers.

'Put a hole in him if he tries anything,' I advised her.

Smithers said nothing. His face looked like a corpse under the blue interior lights. Usher was busy up front. The throbbing of the engine increased. There was a crackle like someone revving up a motor-cycle and choking blue smoke filled the interior of the tank. I could see little points of light lancing out ahead and striking sparks from the ground. Figures were running and falling.

Usher gave them a last burst with the machine-gun and then reversed the Sherman out of the wreckage; bricks and concrete crunched to powder under the immense weight of the hardened steel tracks. Timber and other debris clanged on to the closed turret, reverberating like we were in a sardine can. Looking round at our cramped figures I guess we were at that. Usher idled the engine.

'Your turn, Mike,' he said. I got up into the padded seat, found I could see everything in the mirror. Usher showed me how to work the accelerator, the clutch mechanism and other controls. He put my hands on two massive levers which controlled the tracks. By retarding one I could slew the monster round and change direction.

'I hope you know what you're letting yourself in for,' I said, as we lurched experimentally forward.

'You're doing great, boy,' he said insincerely. 'If you hear a lot of banging take no notice. I'm going on the six-pounder.'

He opened the turret hatch while I concentrated on getting the Sherman across the broken ground in order to skirt the blazing truck park. The levers shuddered and vibrated under my hands as the tons of armour picked up speed. I could see a line of figures bringing up a machine-gun on a tripod. Usher's feet were dangling somewhere near my head now.

'Steady her up, Mike,' he shouted. We hadn't had time to fix up the headphone system and Usher didn't know how it worked anyway. I did my best, there was a sharp crack, we all coughed in the sudden gush of smoke which filled the interior and a flash of red flame bloomed ten yards to the right of the cluster round the machine-gun. Usher shouted with pleasure. There was a clang as a hot brass shell case clanged down into the interior of the Sherman. More smoke rushed out of the breech of the six-pounder as Usher swung it open. He operated the shell-hoist with the foot pedal and rammed another shell smoothly home.

The gun cracked again while I was putting the Sherman into a long climb up a concrete slope past the truck park, but I couldn't seem to control her properly; the side of a water tank was coming up fast.

'I can't hold her,' I called again.

'Don't worry,' said Usher imperturbably. 'She was built for knocking buildings over.'

'I could do with one of these for the traffic in L.A. these days,' I told him.

We took a swipe out of the metal struts holding up the tower as we went by; Usher came down from the turret rather suddenly and clanged the lid behind him. A noise like a thousand bathtubs collapsing made a hollow booming behind us.

'Christ! That was close,' Usher said.

'You told me not to worry,' I said. He didn't answer that one. I glanced round quickly at the girl and the professor; Smithers sat with his trembling hands at his sides. We shouldn't have any trouble with him.

A moment later Usher fired again. There were flashes ahead and more figures running. A jeep caught fire at the edge of my mirror area. More significant, I saw one or two private cars making their way down the road I knew led to the frontier post Trygon had set up. I was driving in great style as we came up to the forecourt of the President's Headquarters. Usher ejected another shell case and re-loaded. He turned to the cowering form of Smithers.

'Where's the meeting?'

'Not the Conference Room,' Smithers said. 'The main study on the ground floor.'

By this time I was putting the tank up a set of shallow concrete steps at the front of the building; the levers were vibrating so hard in my hands that I thought the whole box of tricks would come apart. Usher put one shot from the six-pounder through an upper storey window and then neatly punched out the front door. Bullets spanged angrily on the hardened-steel armour of the Sherman. The sentries in front of the building spread out in all directions as Usher gave them a spray with the machine-gun. The concourse was deserted.

I managed to disengage the clutch and we sat with throbbing engine at the head of the steps, the six-pounder trained on the hole where the main door had been. Usher got down from his bucket seat and caught General

Smithers by the collar. He put the barrel of his pistol against the sweating man's forehead.

'Your information had better be correct, my dear,' he said pleasantly. The first light of dawn was spilling in through the slits of the Sherman; apart from a few muffled explosions from far away behind us it was comparatively quiet. Compared with what it had been, of course. The girl's face looked drawn and tired but she managed to give me a slow smile. The old man was sleeping the sleep of absolute fatigue.

Usher smiled at Smithers.

'You're due for a Presidential citation for this.'

I put in the clutch, took a firm grip on the levers and the Sherman headed for the main door of Trygon's Headquarters.

Chapter Nineteen

Death of a President

1

The double doors of Trygon's study went down before the Sherman with a crash like the end of the world and we were through in a choking cloud of brickdust and plaster. I disengaged the clutch and kept the engine running. Usher got up in the turret and kept the men in the room covered with his pistol. When the dust cleared I could see a long table like you find in a boardroom and the impassive figures of the Chinese delegates. They'd been joined by three others; there were now five in all. They stood in back of the table, with Mr Pen Ching in the middle.

They'd been alerted by the gunfire some time earlier; I noticed ceiling plaster was down in several places and at least three of the big floor to ceiling windows at the back of the room were in splinters. The charred remains of documents still smouldered in a series of glazed ashtrays set out along the table's length. There was a leather briefcase lying on a blotter at the centre of the table; its contents were so bulky that it bulged. Several other cases were piled around the table edge. Two men in the uniforms of captains stood with naked revolvers in their hands in front of the windows. They licked their lips nervously as they eyed the Sherman and waited for instructions.

President Trygon sat in the place of honour, with the briefcases in front of him, next to Mr Pen Ching. His great pink domed head was lowered on to his arms and he looked like he was asleep. Then he raised his head and the silver eyepatch and the red-rimmed eye behind the monocle made him look like Cyclops. Waves of force seemed to come out of his powerful body.

I'd never actually heard anybody grind their teeth but I could swear Trygon's were grinding as he asked Usher with controlled fury, 'You have, I take it, a good explanation of your behaviour this morning, Colonel Usher?'

It was the understatement of the year but I had to admire Trygon's manner under the circumstances. He clenched his jaw and again I fancied I could hear bone creak in his powerful mouth, even above the throbbing of the Sherman's engine. Usher's voice rang out against the noise of distant explosions.

'You've just been invaded by the United States, Mr President! This is an abdication ceremony.'

He turned to the impassive figures of the Chinese. 'I would advise you to keep out of this, Mr Pen Ching. We have no direct quarrel with you.'

The leader of the Chinese delegation bowed. There was a glint of irony in his eyes.

'You are suggesting, I presume, that we accompany you to the civil authorities?'

'You catch on quickly, Mr Pen Ching,' said Usher breezily. 'What their attitude will be, I can't say, of course. Probably nothing more than questioning followed by repatriation. Leave the satchels, naturally.'

Mr Pen Ching stood lost in thought. Trygon sat on as though carved in stone.

Then the Chinese bowed again. 'As you say,

Colonel. We do not seem to have much choice. What do you advise?'

'That you withdraw to whatever transport you came in and follow us on down. If you haven't got a car you'll find plenty to spare outside.'

'Thank you, Colonel Usher.' Mr Pen Ching motioned to his colleagues and the five men filed out. When the last of their footsteps had died away Trygon stood up. His silver eye-patch winked blankly as he looked up at Usher in the tank turret.

'There is only one penalty for a man who has ruined the work of twenty years and who has added treachery to his crimes against the state, Colonel Usher,' he said. 'And that is death.'

He fell to the floor behind the big table as the guards at the back of the room levelled their revolvers and opened fire; blue smoke obscured the scene and the snick of bullets ricochetting off the armour plate came to my ears. I heard Smithers give a smothered exclamation but I saw that April Dawn had him firmly covered. Usher sagged in the turret; I looked up and saw scarlet spreading across his uniform, spilling from the ends of his fingers. His body jerked convulsively and then he collapsed. I got to the button of the machine gun, swung the barrel, spitting flame and smoke in a wide arc. One of the captains dropped, as though cut in half by the concentration of bullets. The other ducked low and rushed at the Sherman, below the trajectory of the machine gun. I waited until he was almost up to the turret and then shot him between the eyes with the Smith-Wesson. I glanced up and saw no sign of life from Usher. I started to get angry then.

I saw that Trygon had gotten off the floor. He scooped up the briefcase and several others with it. He looked like a crab as he scuttled across the room. He dropped two of the cases and came back. I got off a burst then but the gun suddenly jammed. It had been given heavy use that morning. Trygon stopped and picked up the cases as I put the clutch in. The Sherman shuddered, almost stalled and then I hit the accelerator. Trygon turned, his pistol up. He emptied the chamber straight at my driving visor but I was closing the range and the bullets glanced harmlessly off the heavy plating. He threw the gun at the turret as the Sherman was right on top of him.

He slipped away as I increased the acceleration. I saw bills start falling from the open mouth of the briefcase. They seemed like a symbol of his greed as they laid a trail of dollars across the floor behind him. The briefcase slipped again and dropped. His avarice was too much for him. He stopped to scoop it up, saw the Sherman looming over him. His thin scream was cut off by the roar of the engine as I accelerated hard and closed my eyes. There was the slightest imperceptible bump and the scream was cut off.

I reversed across the room from the broken mash that had been a man. A silver eye-patch and a gold monocle lay intact nearby. They caught the light for the last time as I backed out the main door, leaving a carmine trail across the study behind me. Usher woke up then. Clasping his wounded arm he clambered down from the turret. I stopped the Sherman and looked for something to staunch the hole in his biceps.

When I had stopped the bleeding Usher went back in the turret again and surveyed the growing flames across the compound. The main Headquarters building was burning now.

'I claim back this territory on behalf of the United States of America,' he said flippantly. He started tearing braid and medals off his chest.

2

We rolled down the highway towards Tintoretto Canyon in great style. Mr Pen Ching's car stayed close behind us. Usher leaned against the side of the tank and smoked the cigarette I'd given him.

'Thanks for everything, Mike,' he said.

'It was a great team,' I told him. 'Next time you want to start a Palace Revolution, let me know.'

'All the same,' said Usher, 'there's going to be problems, explaining to the civil authoritites. A pity all that money got burned.'

'It didn't,' I said. I pointed down near my feet where Trygon's stuffed briefcases, bill for bill intact, were stacked. 'I haven't yet got to the stage where I can see good money go burn. Besides, it belongs to Red China, doesn't it?'

Usher grinned. Even April Dawn and Professor Hilton were smiling. General Smithers was the only one with nothing to laugh about. Despite the sunrise I felt a little weary myself. I was reconstructing the scene when I had to explain the whole set-up to McGiver and Captain Dan Tucker. I wondered whether Bishop was still sitting by his phone. And what Stella had been doing. I didn't have to wonder long. We crashed through the customs barrier and I saw that Stella had thought it over and had decided not to wait. I could always rely on Stella.

The rising sun was full on my face as we rumbled past the house called Shangri-La and down the main highway to meet the high-pitched sirens of the L.A. Police Department prowl cars. We hadn't gone more than another hundred yards before I could see Dan Tucker's pop-eyes in the leading vehicle. Stella's gold head was beside him.

Chapter Twenty

Star Witness

1

It took three days to sort things out. I figured it would be better if I booked a room at County Police H.Q. Dan Tucker was as rough as I'd thought he'd be. But then I guess he had a right. Stella came down with me every day. So far I figured I'd made a net loss of several hundred dollars on the case, counting wasted time and such-like.

The police had exhumed the bodies of the truck drivers from Trygon's canyon graves and even Davidson had finally admitted that Bishop had gotten on to something important. The one bright spot was the aerial pictures I'd taken with Bill Swain; the F.B.I. had impounded those and I gathered that the C.I.A. had taken them over in their turn. April Dawn and her uncle were as good as new and all the stray bodies had been rounded up.

Judging by what the papers printed, the police and the higher authorities had gone a pretty good cover-up job, but it was going to take some time to sort out spheres of influence so far as the killings were concerned. Gaton—I had difficulty realizing he wasn't Usher—had done the trick here; he was keeping a watching brief for the F.B.I. and it was mainly thanks to him that I hadn't lost my licence. The lecture I got from Captain Dan Tucker almost made me wish I had.

Most of Trygon's boys had scattered and Smithers was the star witness; he was making the most of it. They'd let him keep his uniform and he was putting up a great front for the camera boys the last time I saw him. Then the police photographer, a man named Martin, came in to take his own set for records. Smithers was covered in yards of gold braid and his flabby features were alive with self-importance.

'I want to look beautiful,' he told Martin as the photographer focussed up.

'I'm a photographer, not a plastic surgeon,' Martin told him.

Gaton and I went out. We stopped on the steps outside County Police H.Q. He gave me a tough, horny hand to shake. His scar looked a vivid white in the sunshine.

'I don't suppose we'll be meeting again, Mr Faraday,' he said, 'But I'll never forget you.'

I laughed. 'You don't suppose I'm likely to disremember you? No 1 Execution Squad?'

Gaton smiled shyly and shook hands with Stella. 'Hang on to him, miss,' he said. 'They don't make them like that any more.'

'Don't worry, Mr Gaton,' Stella said, looking up at me, smiling. 'I'll take good care of him.'

Cardinal Bishop was mumbling at my elbow. His pasty face was shiny with sweat and his eyes looked like two hot coals. He'd had his licence suspended for three months for not reporting the truckie's body to the proper authorities. Seeing that I'd done the same I thought it was a tough break, but Tucker had to take it out on somebody.

'How's a guy to live?' he complained. 'Davidson's fee was swallowed in expenses and I finish up with a heavy debit.'

'Don't forget you owe me fifty per-cent,' I said mildly.

Bishop went up like a straw-rick in the dry season. 'I've made nothing on this deal,' he whined. 'I'm even out of pocket on my cab fare down here every day. And that's another two dollars back this afternoon. I do all the footwork and finish up with nothing.'

I left him there. I went down the steps with Stella, breathing in the warm air, the sun bright and strong on my face, looking at Stella's smile and thinking of other things than money.

'You couldn't lend me a couple of bucks?' Bishop called after me with a flash of gold teeth.

I went on down the steps.

'Don't bleed on me,' I said.

We hope you have enjoyed this Large Print book. Other Chivers Press or Thorndike Press Large Print books are available at your library or directly from the publishers.

For more information about current and forthcoming titles, please call or write, without obligation, to:

Chivers Large Print
published by BBC Audiobooks Ltd
St James House, The Square
Lower Bristol Road
Bath BA2 3BH
UK
email: bbcaudiobooks@bbc.co.uk
www.bbcaudiobooks.co.uk

OR

Thorndike Press
295 Kennedy Memorial Drive
Waterville
Maine 04901
USA
www.gale.com/thorndike
www.gale.com/wheeler

All our Large Print titles are designed for easy reading, and all our books are made to last.

1	26	51	76	101	126	151	238	341	488
2	27	52	77	102	127	152	241	355	499
3	28	53	78	103	128	153	242	357	500
4	29	54	79	104	129	154	243	363	509
5	30	55	80	105	130	155	244	375	511
6	31	56	81	106	131	156	249	380	517
7	32	57	82	107	132	160	250	383	519
8	33	58	83	108	133	164	252	393	523
9	34	59	84	109	134	166	257	396	529
10	35	60	85	110	135	167	259	400	534
11	36	61	86	111	136	172	262	403	538
12	37	62	87	112	137	175	268	405	544
13	38	63	88	113	138	180	269	413	552
14	39	64	89	114	139	182	272	417	554
15	40	65	90	115	140	183	273	435	558
16	41	66	91	116	141	189	274	440	565
17	42	67	92	117	142	192	279	447	566
18	43	68	93	118	143	195	285	451	570
19	44	69	94	119	144	203	288	452	574
20	45	70	95	120	145	208	299	453	575
21	46	71	96	121	146	220	310	460	583
22	47	72	97	122	147	227	312	461	595
23	48	73	98	123	148	233	317	478	601
24	49	74	99	124	149	234	324	479	619
25	50	75	100	125	150	237	331	486	624